ECHOES IN THE WIND

Books by Beverly Lewis

THE CUL-DE-SAC KIDS
Children's Fiction

The Double Dabble Surprise	Pickle Pizza
The Chicken Pox Panic	Mailbox Mania
The Crazy Christmas Angel Mystery	The Mudhole Mystery
No Grown-ups Allowed	Fiddlesticks
Frog Power	The Crabby Cat Caper
The Mystery of Case D. Luc	Tarantula Toes
The Stinky Sneakers Mystery	Green Gravy
Backyard Bandit Mystery	

SUMMERHILL SECRETS
Youth Fiction

Whispers Down the Lane	A Cry in the Dark
Secret in the Willows	House of Secrets
Catch a Falling Star	Echoes in the Wind
Night of the Fireflies	

HOLLY'S HEART SERIES
Youth Fiction

Holly's First Love	Straight-A Teacher
Secret Summer Dreams	The "No-Guys" Pact
Sealed With A Kiss	Little White Lies
The Trouble With Weddings	Freshmen Frenzy
California Christmas	Mystery Letters
Second-Best Friend	Eight Is Enough
Good-bye, Dressel Hills	It's a Girl Thing

THE HERITAGE OF LANCASTER COUNTY
Adult Fiction

The Shunning	The Confession

ECHOES IN THE WIND

Beverly Lewis

BETHANY HOUSE PUBLISHERS
MINNEAPOLIS, MINNESOTA 55438

Echoes in the Wind
Copyright © 1997
Beverly Lewis

Cover illustration by Chris Ellison

Published by Bethany House Publishers
A Ministry of Bethany Fellowship, Inc.
11300 Hampshire Avenue South
Minneapolis, Minnesota 55438

Printed in the United States of America.

Library of Congress Cataloging-in-Publication Data

Lewis, Beverly, 1949–
   Echoes in the wind / by Beverly Lewis.
      p. cm. — (Summerhill secrets ; 7)
   Summary: A skating accident during Christmas vacation helps
fourteen-year-old Merry reassess her feelings for Jon, her high
school classmate, and Levi, the elder son of her Amish neighbors.
   ISBN 1–55661–873–5
   [1. Interpersonal relations—Fiction. 2. Christian life—
Fiction.] I. Title. II. Series: Lewis, Beverly, 1949–
SummerHill secrets ; 7.
PZ7.L5864Ef   1997
[Fic]—dc21   97–4707
                                            CIP
                                            AC

For Christine Dennis,
my young writer/friend,
who has much in common
with Merry Hanson.

And . . .

for Becky Byler,
my little Amish friend,
who has more in common
with Rachel Zook.

BEVERLY LEWIS is a speaker, teacher, and the best-selling author of the HOLLY'S HEART series. She has written over thirty books for adults, teens, and children. Many of her articles and stories have appeared in the nation's top magazines.

Beverly is a member of The National League of American Pen Women and the Society of Children's Book Writers and Illustrators. She and her husband, Dave, along with their three teenagers, live in Colorado. She fondly remembers their cockapoo named Cuddles, who used to snore to Mozart!

Friendships multiply joys. . . .

Handbook of Proverbs, 1855

ONE

"If I die before my mom gets to come home," Chelsea Davis said one wintry afternoon, "will you tell her how much I loved her?"

I stopped playing with my kitten, Lily White, and stared at my long-time friend. "You're *not* dying, and your mom'll be home soon. You'll see."

"But it's taking forever to get her well again." She scooted over the living room floor, going to sit cross-legged in front of our stone fireplace. Her auburn hair fell halfway down her back as she stared into the flames. Turning, she motioned for me to join her.

I abandoned Lily White, who had succumbed to a cat-nap, and went to sit on the rug next to Chelsea. The warmth from the fire made my face all warm and rosy.

We fell silent, becoming almost drowsy as the blaze crackled and snapped before us. It was the coldest December day in twenty years, or so the noon weather-man had just announced. And I was absolutely thrilled that my friend had come to stay for the weekend. Because, for more than one reason, I was worried about her.

Recently, Chelsea and I had become close friends. Probably because we'd lived through a real-life trauma—the nightmarish event of her mother running away to join a cult group.

Back in October, Mrs. Davis had made friends with an outgoing couple and, unknowingly, had fallen under their spell and that of their leader. She'd even taken some sort of oath and gone away to live at a compound, leaving Chelsea and her dad alone—and terribly hurt and confused. Now Mrs. Davis was being rehabilitated, and the family hoped she'd be released in time for the holidays.

"When was the last time you heard from your mom?" I asked.

"Last week." Her eyes grew serious. "But she didn't wanna talk much. I don't think she likes the phone—one of her new phobias, maybe."

"So why don't you tell her how you feel in a letter?"

"That I love her?" She seemed surprised.

"Or send a card that says it for you."

Chelsea turned back to watch the fire. "I don't know."

"It's only a suggestion."

Nodding, she continued. "How would *you* feel if your mom went off and lost her mind?"

I took a deep breath. "I really don't know."

Truth was, Chelsea's mom was as sane as anyone in the Lancaster County area. She'd been brainwashed, though, and as my dad (who's a doctor) had explained to me, *sometimes these things take a long time.*

Not wanting to stir up more sorrow in my friend, I

steered the conversation to other things. "Did I tell you? Levi Zook is coming home."

"For Christmas?" Her sea-green eyes brightened. "Since when?"

"Well, he's back from his overseas mission. I know that much."

"Hey, I think you've been holding out on me," she insisted. "Did he write or something?"

I tried not to grin.

"Well, what are we waiting for? Let's have a look at the letter." She was getting a bit pushy now. First morbid . . . now bossy. Which was worse?

"You don't *really* want to read it, do you?" I said.

But she saw through me. "Okay, Mer, if that's the way you wanna play it, fine." And with that, she got up and ran for the stairs.

Of course I was trailing close behind. I didn't want Chelsea to actually find Levi's letter—let alone read what the former Amish boy had written.

Levi Zook was probably the most sincere and loyal seventeen-year-old guy I'd ever known. But then, I didn't really know many boys his age, except for my own brother, Skip, who was in his first year of college.

Actually, Levi and I—and the other Zook children— had grown up together. Our properties shared the same boundary—a thick grove of willow trees. Having grown up in an Old Order Amish family, Levi was fun loving and hardworking. He was also very persistent. Seemed to know exactly what he wanted out of life.

"So where's the letter?" Chelsea demanded, sporting a grin.

I closed the door to my bedroom. "How about if I just summarize it for you?"

"Forget it! I want details—the latest in the ongoing romantic saga between—"

"Romantic? Levi and I aren't . . . uh, together or anything."

"Could've fooled me." She sat at my desk, flashing a sneaky smile as, slowly, she pulled out the narrow drawer. "Is this it? Is this your hiding place?"

I folded my arms and watched, refusing her a single clue. Leaning against the door, I waited.

Naturally, she wasn't anywhere near the spot where I kept private letters and things. But I was surprised to see that she had found something. Something I'd completely forgotten about.

"Well, what do we have here?" She held up a note from Jonathan Klein. It was the one he'd passed to me during math class on Thursday, just two days ago.

I knew if I didn't respond, Chelsea would think she'd discovered a gold mine. "Oh, that." I pushed my hair back over my shoulder nonchalantly. "Go ahead, have a look."

She moved her lips, probably trying to decipher his alliterated words, then frowned, apparently puzzled. "Does he always write like this?"

I wasn't about to divulge Jon's and my big secret—our ongoing word game. Frequently, we talked to each other in what we called alliteration-eze, trying to see who could think faster off the top of the head. Usually, it was Jon—that's why I'd secretly named him the Alliteration Wizard.

"Oh, you know Jon," I said, hoping she'd drop the subject.

She glanced at the note again, then waved it in a mocking manner. "Seems to me the next few weeks could be *very* interesting around here."

I didn't have to think twice to know what she meant. The fact was, both Levi and Jon would be breathing the same brisk Pennsylvania air this Christmas.

My one and only hope was that they wouldn't show up at my house on the exact same day.

TWO

After supper, Chelsea did some more poking around. "C'mon, Mer, won'tcha give me at least one little hint?" She opened the door to my walk-in closet, then glanced over her shoulder at me. "Well . . . am I hot or cold?"

Honestly, she was very warm; in fact, close to stepping into forbidden territory. "Let's just say you're downright nosy!"

We burst out laughing, and much to my relief, she closed the closet door and came to sit on the bed beside me. "You really don't want me to read it, do you, Merry?"

I ignored the question, wandering over to the bookcase to search through volumes of old poetry. "Here," I said, thumbing through Longfellow. "Now this is truly cool."

Hearing her exhale, I knew she was restless—my being so evasive and all. "What's this got to do with Levi Zook?" she insisted.

"Just wait. You'll see." I planted myself in the middle of the room and cleared my throat. "I want you to hear a beautiful passage from *Evangeline.*"

"Oh, real sweet, Mer," she retorted, folding her arms. "How boring can you get?"

"No . . . listen. It's incredible, really." I glanced at her, waiting for the fake scowl to fade. "Are you ready?"

"Do I have a choice?"

I held the book open and began to read, " 'And, when the echoes had ceased, like a sense of pain was the silence.' "

She gazed up at me incredulously. "Who wrote that?"

"Henry Wadsworth Longfellow."

"Read it again," she said softly.

I did and, by the serene look on her face, knew Chelsea had actually enjoyed it.

"What's it mean?" she asked.

Returning the book to the shelf, I gave her my two cents' worth. "I suppose you could read into it whatever you want to. But for me, it's about Levi. I mean, there are many happy echoes in my mind from our friendship."

"Last summer?"

I nodded. "And before that, because Levi and I are friends from childhood. But they—the echoes—are starting to fade."

Do I dare express something so personal?

Levi had already told me, without mincing words, that I was the girl for him. Only trouble was, he was off at a Mennonite college in Virginia now, and I was a freshman at James Buchanan High. Besides, we'd agreed to remain friends; nothing more. At least for now. Which for me was ideal, especially since I had my heart set on the Alliteration Wizard.

"Are you saying you're suffering because of Levi's silence?" Chelsea asked.

"Well, he hasn't written for weeks. But then, he's been down in South America building a church."

She stretched her arms high over her head. "Whoa, I'm totally confused. I mean, the way you look at Jon Klein sometimes . . . what's that about?"

"What?"

She giggled. "C'mon, Mer, you know what I'm talking about."

"No, I don't. And I think it's time you spill it out!"

She jumped off the bed and started pulling on my arm. "Come sit down and stop showing off, and maybe I will."

I probably *was* overdoing the dramatics—reading highbrow poetry and all, especially to a down-home girl like Chelsea. Actually, we were both country girls. "Okay, I'm sitting. So talk."

And she did. Told me what she'd been observing every morning in the hallways of James Buchanan High. "Jon's always hanging out at your locker. And you . . . you're always soaking it up."

"What do you mean, soaking? Aren't friends supposed to pay attention to each other?" It was a pitiful comeback.

"But this thing you two are always doing," she added. "It just looks so . . . so weird."

"What? What's weird?"

She pulled on a strand of her hair, pausing for a moment before going on. "Oh, I don't know, you always end up staring at him, Mer, not saying a word—like you're love-struck or something."

"Oh, that. I know exactly what you're saying. But it's not what you think!"

Her eyes bore into me. "So, what *is* it?"

I fell over onto the bed in a torrent of giggles. What Chelsea didn't know was that each morning before school, Jon would show up at my locker with some sort of clever greeting. Always alliterated, actually.

He expected me to fire back something similar in response. So what Chelsea had termed as pining over Jon was nothing more than mere concentration on my part.

"What's so funny?" she demanded. "Are you completely nuts over two guys? Is that it?"

This was a curious comment, and one I certainly didn't want to explore further. Not with Chelsea. Probably not with anyone.

I grabbed one of my sham pillows and playfully began flinging it at her. "You ask way too many questions."

Unexpectedly, she followed suit, walloping me good with the other bed pillow. "I must be right!" she hollered gleefully. And the first pillow fight of the weekend had begun.

But Chelsea was *not* right. Not even close. I have to admit that it was I who liked Jon—liked him a lot. But it was Levi who liked me.

❧   ❧

During family devotions, Chelsea listened as Dad read the Bible. She surprised me by being attentive. This was the atheist girlfriend who'd resisted everything I'd ever said about God or the Bible up until a few months ago. Tomorrow she was going to attend Sunday school and church with me and my family. Not for the first time, either.

Later, when we changed into our pajamas upstairs, Chelsea asked me to pray with her. "You know, about my mom," she said with trusting eyes. "More than anything, I want her back home for Christmas."

"Sure, I'll pray." We knelt beside my bed, surrounded by Shadrach, Meshach, Abednego, and Lily White, my four wonderful cats. Folding my hands, I began. "Dear Lord, thank you for being with Chelsea's mom and—"

"And for getting her this far safely," Chelsea cut in.

I smiled, my eyes still closed. "We know you have a plan for her . . . and for the whole Davis family," I continued. "We're counting on you to work things out."

She was quick to add, "And if you don't mind, could you please bring my mom home in time for . . . for your birthday?"

I was so delighted, I could hardly end the prayer. Instead, Chelsea jumped right in and finished for me. "Amen, and thanks for hearing Merry's and my prayer."

Turning, I gave her a hug. "Hey, you're good. Is this a first?"

She dipped her head, looking sheepish. "First time praying out loud, yeah."

"So . . . you've been talking to God silently sometimes?"

"At home in my room."

Getting up, I arranged the cat quartet on top of my blue-striped comforter toward the foot of the bed. "I'm glad you told me, Chels." I was going to let her have my bed for the night. The floor and my sleeping bag were just fine for me.

"Now that you know one of *my* secrets, how about if you tell me about that letter of yours?" She was steadfast and persistent. Almost as determined as Levi!

Before going to the closet, I swept my hair back into a loose ponytail, securing it with a rubber band. Then I went to locate the pinkish shoe box nestled on the middle shelf of my closet near my camera equipment and pulled it down. "Okay. You wanna know about Levi . . . here goes." I felt surprisingly comfortable with what I'd decided to do.

Sifting through the small box, I found his latest letter and handed it to my friend. By the eager look on Chelsea's face, she was itching to have a peek. Maybe if she read it for herself she would see that *I* was not the one pushing for romance! Not in the least.

THREE

"Okay with you if I read out loud?" Chelsea wore a triumphant look.

"Just don't be too loud." I glanced at the door. "You know how a mother can be sometimes." Suddenly, I realized how foolish my comment was. From what Chelsea had been saying all along, she'd give anything to have *her* mother around.

Chelsea began reading: " 'My dear Merry,' " Stopping for a second, she hinted a smile. "Is this how he always starts?"

I shrugged. "Read it. Don't analyze it."

She went on. " 'I realize it may seem like a long time since you've gotten a letter from me, and it has been. But all this time I've been helping build a church in Bolivia with other Mennonite students.

" 'Please, Merry, don't be thinking that I haven't thought of you every day, though, since leaving SummerHill.' "

She paused momentarily, gazing at me with quizzical

eyes. "This guy's crazy about you!"

"Shh! Keep your voice down," I reminded her.

"Yeah, yeah . . . because your mom's gonna think Levi's coming home to propose if she gets wind of it, right?"

"There's no chance of a proposal. I'm one-hundred-percent-amen sure about that."

Chelsea chuckled at my pet phrase. "Sounds like you're mighty positive."

"I'm *only* fourteen. Levi's got better sense."

"Well," she shot back, "everyone knows the Amish marry young."

"But he's not Amish anymore." I motioned for her to continue the letter. "He's Mennonite now."

She smiled a taunting smile, then found her place and continued. " 'The Lord willing, I'll be coming home December 20th to spend Christmas with my family. I want to see you, Merry. Will that suit you?' "

By now, Chelsea was bouncing up and down on my bed, reacting to the quaint, folksy sound of his letter, no doubt.

"Calm down," I said. "It's no big deal."

But she was beside herself with glee, waving the letter around. "I can't believe you're not freaked out about this. I mean, this Levi-person is definitely in love with you, Merry Hanson!"

I dashed over and snatched the letter out of her hand. "Let me see that!" Scanning through it, I especially scrutinized the remainder.

Remember, if it won't work out for us to visit together before or during Christmas, we'll have plenty of time to talk afterward. I'll be in the Lancaster area well into the New Year. God bless you always, Merry.

With greatest affection,
Levi Zook

It was out of the question. No one was going to read the ending of this letter! Quickly, I returned it to the safety of the envelope. "I think you've had enough for one night," I stated.

"Hey!" Chelsea wailed. "Don't do this to me!"

The noise brought an almost instant knock on my bedroom door. "Girls, girls, it's getting late," Mom's voice crept through.

"Sorry," I called. "We were just going to bed."

"Don't you wish," Chelsea whispered, eyeing me.

"We *are*," I insisted after the sound of footsteps faded away.

"Aw, don't be such a party pooper," she whined.

"This isn't a party. Besides, I'm tired." And I was ticked, too. Chelsea was being a real pain. I turned out the light and wiggled down into my sleeping bag. "'Night."

"Don't be so sensitive" came her reply.

I huffed a bit. "Well, I am, so get over it."

A few moments passed, and my eyes began to adjust to the dark room. I wondered if I'd been too short with her.

Then Chelsea's voice broke the silence. "Hey, I'm sorry. Okay?"

"Sure. See you in the morning."

❧   ❧

Sunday breakfast was served promptly at eight-thirty. Dad—not Mom—expected us to be at the table without delay. Which meant both Chelsea and I were rushing around taking turns in the shower.

Dad had always been a stickler for promptness, especially on Sundays. To him, it was better to show up for church half an hour early than to be ten minutes late.

When Chelsea and I made our entrance into the kitchen, he peered over his newspaper briefly, sporting a stubby growth of whiskers as he sat at the head of the table. "Good morning, girls."

"Morning," we said in unison.

Mom served up her best blueberry muffins along with scrambled eggs, bacon, and a side dish of cantaloupe. Chelsea gave me a sideways glance, eyes wide.

"Mom doesn't mess around at mealtime," I said, loud enough for Mom to hear.

She smiled, coming over to the table with fresh butter from the Zooks' farm and a dish of whipped cream for the muffins. "Merry's right," she said, serving Dad first. "Always remember: Good eaters make good citizens."

To that, Dad closed his paper, clucking as Mom sat across from him. "I don't know about the 'good citizens' part," he said. "But it never hurts to eat heartily now and then."

Chelsea bowed her head along with the rest of us when Dad said the table blessing. Having her in the house

like this—seeing her eager to join in with our family rou-
tine—encouraged me. I couldn't wait to tell Levi about
the changes happening in her. Maybe it was the one thing
we would feel comfortable talking about while he was
home. Back last spring, he'd agreed to pray for Chelsea,
as had Jon Klein and several other of my church friends.

And amazing things had begun to take place. In fact,
the girl was a walking, breathing turnaround. And now,
sitting beside her at our family table, I was beginning to
feel truly sorry about the way I'd cut her off last night.

After the prayer and a quick morning devotional,
Mom poured orange juice for everyone. "I almost forgot,
Merry," she said. "Rachel Zook stopped by earlier."

"She did?"

"She wants you to visit her sometime this afternoon."

I glanced at Chelsea. "Wanna see an authentic Amish
dairy farm?"

"Cool," she replied.

"Good. Then we'll go right after dinner."

Dad stirred sugar into his coffee and mentioned a recent rumor he'd heard. "Is it true that Levi Zook is coming home for Christmas?"

He was asking *me*!

Chelsea smirked, no doubt dying to see how I handled
myself.

"Levi's coming home, all right." I was no longer able
to control my smile.

"Oh?" Now it was Mom's turn to perk up her ears.

I flashed a warning to Chelsea. Now wasn't the time

for her to blurt something out about the boy's "sweet" letter.

After a gulp of juice, I explained, "Rachel's probably planning something special for him. Who knows? A welcome-home party *would* be nice." It was an attempt to divert the focus of the conversation, even though I knew well and good the Amish weren't much for throwing parties.

Dad resumed his coffee drinking and—thank goodness—seemed to be losing interest.

Mom wasn't as easy to sidetrack. "How is it that you know all this?" she asked.

Chelsea was anything but discreet in her reaction to Mom's pointed question. She coughed and nearly choked! And if I hadn't been in complete control of *my* wits, I'd have sent her a fiery dart with my eyes.

Or worse.

FOUR

That afternoon, we bundled up in the warmest clothing we could find. Chelsea, who hadn't anticipated the snowy trek to our neighbors' farmhouse when she'd packed, borrowed a scarf and heavy mittens from Mom. We were so heavily wrapped in layers, we honestly felt like lunar astronauts. Laughing, we lumbered down the long front walk, then on toward SummerHill Lane.

I didn't even think of taking the shortcut to Rachel's house this time. But I told Chelsea about the secret place deep in the willow grove, now buried in snow, far back from the road.

"Really? There's a secret place in there?" She shielded her eyes from the sun, looking.

"It's impossible to see from here."

"Does Levi know about it?" she teased.

I shook my head, breathing hard as we turned into Zooks' long, private lane. "The willow grove has always been Rachel's and my place, I guess you could say."

"I can't wait to see where she lives."

"Rachel Zook might sound a little different—I mean,

the way she talks and stuff," I explained.

"I remember." Then Chelsea reminded me that she'd already met Rachel. "She came to my house with the cocker spaniel puppy in October . . . after Mom left us."

"Oh, that's right." I breathed in the icy, damp air. "So . . . what did you think of Rachel?"

"Well, for starters, I think she needs some help choosing her wardrobe." She snickered. "Other than that, she's okay."

"All Amish women dress that way," I said.

Chelsea hurried to keep up with me. "What's she gonna think, you bringing a stranger over?"

"Oh, you just wait," I said, shivering. "Rachel and her family are the most hospitable folk you could ever want to meet."

"Wow, that's hard to believe. Seems to me that *your* family's the most neighborly around here."

"We try, but the Amish have us beat all to pieces." I turned and headed up the freshly shoveled walk.

Almost immediately, Rachel appeared at the back door, greeting us as she opened it. She was wearing her usual long, dark dress and apron, as well as a white head covering. "*Wilkom!*" she said. "Come on in and get warm." She helped Chelsea with her coat and scarf, smiling broadly when I introduced my friend. "It's real nice to see ya again," Rachel replied. "How's that new puppy of yours?"

Chelsea responded eagerly. "Oh, you oughta see him. He's growing real fast now. And so cute!"

I stood beside the old wood stove, rubbing my hands

together and glancing around at the enormous kitchen, sparkling clean as usual. "Did I ever tell you what Chelsea named the pup?"

Rachel shook her head. "I don't recall."

"She named him Secrets," I volunteered. "Isn't that dear?"

At the mention of the pup's name, little Susie came over from the kitchen table, where she'd been coloring. "I heard ya talkin' about that puppy dog," she said, still holding a crayon.

I gave her a quick hug. "Maybe Secrets can come for a visit sometime. Would you like that?"

Her eyes were bright. "*Jah*. Then he can see his mamma again!"

Abe and Esther Zook glanced up, smiling from their rocking chairs, where they were both reading. It was evident that Sunday—the Lord's Day—particularly a cold, snowy one, was meant to be shared together as a family at the Zooks' farmhouse.

The other children, Nancy, Ella Mae, and Aaron, continued to play their games quietly at the table. Susie, however, had to show off her coloring book before Chelsea and I followed Rachel toward the hallway stairs.

"Make it snappy," her father said. And I knew he wanted all his children gathered around the warm stove in the kitchen.

Soon, I understood why. Rachel's bedroom was practically a deep freeze. Wishing for my coat, I hugged myself. Chelsea did the same.

Almost as soon as the bedroom door shut, Rachel

started jabbering up a storm. "Oh, Merry, didja hear? Our Levi's comin' home for Christmas!"

I nodded, determined not to look at Chelsea. She'd be getting too big a kick out of this.

"Matthew Yoder—my friend down the lane—and I wanna have a skating party on the pond. You know . . . for couples. Wouldja come and be Levi's partner?"

"Uh . . . maybe Levi should have a say in it. You know."

"No, no, it's all a surprise for him," she insisted.

I paused briefly, thinking things over. Chelsea nudged me from behind, and I knew there was no begging off.

"Oh, do come, won'tcha Merry?" Rachel pleaded. "Do it for Levi?" Her heart was set on this. I could see the excitement in her shining eyes.

"Okay," I said. "Sounds like fun. When?"

"How 'bout the day after Levi arrives?" She studied me hard. "That's Saturday, I'm a-thinkin'. And please, keep it a secret from him, won'tcha now?"

Chelsea started to giggle slightly, but my eyes sent a dart of disapproval her way.

"Don't worry. I'll keep it quiet," I promised.

"*Gut,* then it's set." Rachel touched her *kapp,* the white devotional head covering.

Silently, we headed downstairs to the toasty kitchen— a welcome relief in more ways than one.

◦◦ ◦◦

"So . . . the Amish don't throw parties, huh?" Chelsea taunted as we trudged home over the encrusted snow.

"The adults aren't real big on it," I said.

We walked a ways farther, then Chelsea said, "Seems to me, Rachel has more than an inkling how her brother feels about you. Am I right?"

I sighed. "Rachel's got herself a boyfriend now—calls him her *beau*. She must be thinking that everyone else should be in love just 'cause she is."

"Is Rachel's boyfriend Amish?" Her breath hung white in the crisp air.

"You better believe Matthew's Amish. Rachel's bound and determined to marry in her church. In fact, last I heard, they're planning to take instruction classes next summer to prepare for baptism."

"Hmm. I wonder what it would be like," she said.

"What?"

"Oh, being Amish."

I laughed a little. "Well, for a while there, I wondered myself. Even almost convinced myself that I should become Plain—but that was a long time ago."

"Last summer?"

"Uh-huh."

She stared at me. "You've gotta be kidding. All that talk about Levi Zook wanting you to be his girl for the summer—was that for *real*?"

I chuckled. "Surprised even me."

Chelsea adjusted her earmuffs against the wind. "Whoa, Mer, I can almost hear your mom going on about it."

"You don't know the half of it."

"That bad?" she questioned.

"Let's just say it was one of those times in my life when we truly clashed." I left it at that.

We hurried around the side yard, past the gazebo, and toward the back door.

Chelsea seemed to want to pursue the topic, but Mom was watering her African violets in the corner of the kitchen when we walked in. "How are the Zooks?" she asked over her shoulder.

"Oh, you know, it's Sunday, so it's pretty quiet over there," I said.

"Mighty cold, too," Chelsea offered.

Mom turned around, wearing a frown. "Something wrong with their wood stove?"

"Oh, nothing like that," I was quick to say. "But we went upstairs with Rachel for a bit—it was ice cold up there for sure!"

Mom seemed to understand and, fortunately, didn't press for more details.

But Chelsea did. Thank goodness she waited till we were back in my room, though. "Does your mom know you still like Levi?"

"What?"

"C'mon, Mer, you heard me. You're always saying 'what' for no reason."

I shrugged and sat down at my desk across the room from her. Chelsea was right: Saying "what" was a cop out—a bad habit. But *what* could I do about it?

My friend started to gather up her clothes and things. "You know, I have this very strong feeling," she said without looking at me.

Snorting, I went to stand at the window, staring out at the pristine white. Fresh snow covered the field across SummerHill Lane like a wide, thick blanket. "You and your feelings," I muttered.

"Yeah, well, today I was just so sure that you couldn't wait to go visit Rachel," she added.

Not answering, I turned from the window and went around the room finding her brush and perfume and makeup, helping pack her bag.

"You *know* I'm right, Merry." She folded her pajamas and bathrobe. "I mean, you should've seen yourself during church today."

"Now what?"

"You were, uh . . . distracted. A whole lot."

I suppose she had a point, except that I hadn't been thinking about Levi during church. Not at all. And before saying anything to deny it, I piled a handful of her belongings into the overnight case. "Weren't you listening at all yesterday when I read that line from Longfellow?" I said at last.

"Longfellow, short fellow . . . Plain fella. What's the difference?" she tittered.

And that was the beginning of our second and final pillow fight of the weekend.

FIVE

Monday dawned, bringing with it more sub-zero temperatures. A ferocious wind blew out of the east, making me shiver as I waited for the bus in the early morning light. I thought of a poetic phrase, this one by Dickens. *I am always conscious of an uncomfortable sensation now and then when the wind is blowing in the east.*

The old school bus poked its way up SummerHill Lane, puffing white exhaust smoke out the back. The day seemed colder than I ever remembered a Pennsylvania winter, even though, according to the calendar, winter wasn't officially scheduled for another two weeks.

Two more weeks. . . .

Levi would be home soon. How would I act when I saw him again? What would I say? An awkward feeling followed as I thought about seeing him face-to-face.

Then I spotted Abe Zook turning out of his private lane, driving an open sleigh piled with his younger children—all but Rachel, who had already completed the eight grades of school required by the Amish.

One-room Amish schools never had to close for bad

weather around Lancaster. Plain folk were well behind modern technology, but they sure knew how to put ingenuity to good use.

Abe Zook whistled to Apple, one of his three driving horses, and made the turn onto the road. The children waved and called their cheerful "hullos" to me.

Grinning, I was sure Chelsea—if she'd been here to witness it—would have enjoyed this down-home touch of Plain life.

My teeth were chattering by the time the bus creaked to a stop. Half frozen, I stumbled up the steps and into the bus. Chelsea motioned to me, and I slid in next to her.

"Did you see the Zooks' one-horse open sleigh?" I pointed to it through the windshield.

"Hey, cool." Chelsea started singing "Jingle Bells," then told some of the kids behind us about my Amish neighbors. "They're the nicest people, really," she said.

Jon Klein sat several rows ahead of us—nose buried in a book. I tried to recall if he'd looked up about the time I got on. But I knew if he had, I would've remembered.

I stared at the back of his head—his light brown hair was always well-groomed. Jon was the picture of perfection.

Say that with all p's, I told myself, wondering how I'd fare if he ever decided not to stop at my locker for our session of silliness. What then?

I shot a desperate look at Chelsea. She shook her head and shrugged. "Why waste your time on a guy who hardly knows you exist?"

This was a brand-new approach. "Really?" I said.

"Sounds to me like you think I oughta welcome Levi home with open arms."

She twisted her thick auburn locks, worn straight today with bangs feathered off to the side. "At least if you ended up with Levi, you wouldn't have to hire a translator to read his letters," she said, referring back to Jon's note.

"No, but I think I oughta have a genuine call from God first."

She frowned. "What are you saying?"

"Truth is, Levi Zook is studying to be a missionary. He really shouldn't be hanging around with just any girl."

"So you think you're a lousy choice. Is that it?"

"Don't be sarcastic. I *mean* it. Levi should be spending time with girls who feel inclined to become a missionary's wife."

She leaned her elbow on her books and looked straight at me. "You know, Mer, now that I've actually started paying attention to all your God-talk, I think I better tell you something. Not to be mean, but I get the strong feeling you aren't very trusting these days, at least not toward your heavenly Father."

This comment seemed strange coming from Chelsea Davis, the self-proclaimed atheist turned almost believer.

"You're kidding," I heard myself say. "You actually think that?"

"Let's put it this way: Maybe if you spent less time reading that absurd poetry of yours . . ."

She didn't have to finish; I knew what Chelsea meant. Reading the Bible was far more helpful—and important—in the long run.

"Well, if this isn't a switch—you preaching to *me*." I laughed, and wonder of wonders, the Alliteration Wizard turned around and smiled!

❧　❧

Jon began spouting our word game after his usual "Morning, Mistress Merry" greeting. "Whether wind be wintry or wild, we'll while away the wait for warmer weather."

"What?" I said, prolonging closing my locker. With its door gaping wide and Jonathan standing near me, I felt sheltered from the world of school and students. It was only an illusion, of course. "*W*'s, huh? Well, if you ask me, your sentence doesn't make much sense," I was glad to inform him.

His heart-stopping grin caught me off guard. "Better not boast 'bout brilliant comebacks," he replied.

Man, was he good!

"We'll see about that," I said. "Pick a letter. Any letter!"

He thought for a moment, then as he was about to speak, Ashley Horton, our pastor's daughter and probably the prettiest girl in the entire school, came trotting by with Stiggy Eastman, winner of this year's coveted photography contest.

"Hello-o, Merry. Hi, Jon," she cooed, waving.

"Ashley!" The Alliteration Wizard turned suddenly. "You're just the person I need to see." And with that, he dashed off after her, completely forgetting our word game. Forgetting something else, too—a proper good-bye.

⁊⁊   ⁊⁊

All day long, the east wind blew. And with it came echoes—memories of my past days and years as Levi's friend. Was I worrying too much about my next encounter with him? Or was something else bothering me? Anyway, I was truly miserable and told Lissa Vyner, another one of my church friends, about it during P.E.

"You know what's discouraging?" I said. "Every time I think Jon and I might actually have a chance, Ashley comes flouncing along and interferes. It's so-o frustrating."

Lissa pushed her wispy blond hair away from her delicate face, looking at me with wide blue eyes. "Are you praying about this?"

"Like I should be *that* serious," I replied. "I mean, it's not as if I'm even dating yet."

"No, but you do like certain guys. We all do," she said with a perky smile.

I remembered that Jon had been interested in her for a while last spring. "Some of us get all the breaks," I muttered.

She didn't say anything, and we hurried out of the gym locker room, wearing our white shorts and tops, ready for a rousing volleyball game. "How about if I call you tonight?" she said, hurrying off to take her position near the net.

I spotted Ashley Horton on my team. *Oh, great*, I

thought. How was I going to play a decent game with my competition hurling her smile around the court?

Off and on during the match, my mind seemed to play tricks on me. I actually started second-guessing my friendship with Jon. Maybe he was using me . . . could that be all it was? Was I just someone to play his word game? I knew I was truly good as his partner in phrases. And I also knew for a fact that none of the other girls he'd ever liked had been introduced to the Alliteration Game. None!

What did it mean? All the months, and now years, of his amusing himself with my mind?

"Heads up!" The P.E. instructor blew her whistle.

I ducked.

But . . . too late.

The ball slammed into my head. I fell backward, stumbling onto the floor.

"Merry!" I heard Lissa call out.

But in nothing flat, I was sitting up. A goose egg on the back of my head.

I'd hit the floor hard, and the teacher was worried. "We better have the nurse check you out, Merry," she said.

So with Lissa and Ashley on either side of me, I limped dizzily down the hall to the nurse's room.

Served me right, I suppose. Men were a menace to the mind. Hey, I liked that!

And I made a mental note to communicate it to Jon after school.

SIX

The knot on my head turned into a sickening headache by suppertime. Of course my dad made a big deal about checking the pupils of my eyes. "Have to make sure they're dilating normally."

"Do I have a concussion?" I asked, letting Mom baby me by bringing meat loaf, mashed potatoes, and green beans up to my room on a tray.

Flicking on his penlight, Dad shined it in my right eye, then away. "Looks to me like you'll be just fine, honey."

"Why didn't my head hurt earlier?"

Mom pulled up a chair and sat down, watching me eat. "Could be a delayed reaction."

"Perhaps," Dad was saying. "Often the body will kick in just enough adrenaline to carry through the moment of injury and beyond."

"But then, look out—whammy!" I joked but avoided laughing. My head was throbbing too much for that.

When the phone rang, Mom rushed out of the room and down the hall.

Dad winked. "I believe she's expecting a call from your brother."

"Is Skip doing okay now?" I asked.

"If you're referring to his homesickness, yes, I think that may have run its course."

I sipped some hot tea. "Like my headache will, right?"

Dad rubbed his chin thoughtfully. "How did it happen—the volleyball hitting you in the head?"

To tell the truth, I felt uncomfortable spilling out the details to Dad. I mean, he wasn't one to come down hard on stupidity or anything. But I just couldn't bring myself to talk about the state I'd been in during P.E.—contemplating the Alliteration Wizard during a fast-paced volleyball game? C'mon!

"I guess I wasn't paying much attention," I mumbled. Picking up my fork, I proceeded to fill my mouth with mashed potatoes and gravy. That way if he asked additional pointed questions, I'd have plenty of time to think of a genius response while chewing.

"Merry," Mom called from the hallway. "Do you feel up to talking to Lissa Vyner?"

I nodded my answer to Dad, who passed it on to Mom. Soon enough, she brought the cordless phone to me, and my parents made a reluctant exit.

"Hi, Lissa," I said.

"How are you feeling now?"

"Okay, except for this monstrous headache."

"You really got whacked today. What do you expect?"

"I'll live, I guess," I replied.

"Aw, Mer, don't say that." She paused. "Oh, before

I forget, Ashley wants you to know she's worried about you."

"That's nice."

Silence came and went. "Uh . . . you two still aren't—"

"It's nothing to worry about, really," I was quick to say. True, Ashley and I still experienced some friction between us, off and on. Probably because of our mutual interest—both of us had our hearts set on Jon Klein.

Lissa went on. "Will you let me know if there's anything I can do?"

"Thanks, Liss, but I'll be fine."

"Well, if you need homework assignments or anything, have your mom call the school secretary and let me know."

"I really can't miss school tomorrow," I assured her. "But thanks anyway." We said good-bye and hung up, and I resumed eating my supper.

Later, when the pain medication finally took hold, I opened my Bible to the mini-concordance in the back. I searched for the word *echo*, curious to see if it was represented anywhere in the Scriptures. It wasn't.

Then, silly me, I even thought of calling Ashley to ask if she might borrow her father's big concordance to look up the word. Instead, I decided to try a synonym. I looked up the word *answer* in my Bible.

Sure enough, oodles of references. Actually thirty or more. I didn't take time to locate all of them, but I did read Psalm 91, enjoying it for its rhythm and flow—much the way an excellent poem in free verse is written. The part about the angels in verses eleven and twelve always excited me. To think that there were heavenly messengers in charge of protecting us here on earth!

Then I came to the next to the last verse. The verse with the word I was looking for: *Answer.*

God's Word prompted me to pray for Chelsea's mother once again. Surprisingly, when I finished, I wondered if it was too late to call Chelsea herself.

I checked the clock in my room. Eight-thirty. She'd still be up. Swiftly, I dialed her number.

"Davis residence." It was Chelsea's father.

"Hello, Mr. Davis. This is Merry Hanson. May I please speak to Chelsea?"

"Hold on." *Clunk.* He set the phone down hard.

I waited for a moment, feeling uneasy, then Chelsea answered.

"Is everything all right?" I inquired.

She sounded hesitant. "I'm not sure if Daddy wants me telling you this, but my mom just called."

"She did? That's great."

"Well, I don't know. We got the feeling she doesn't wanna come home just yet."

My heart sank. "Oh, Chelsea, I'm so sorry."

"Me too." She sounded as if she might cry. "What if this rehabilitation stuff doesn't work out, Mer? What if she never gets back to her normal self?"

I tried to comfort her. "My dad says it takes longer for some patients. But, please, don't give up. We're praying, remember?"

She was silent for a few seconds. Then—"I really

think your prayers are the only thing keeping us going."

I felt a lump in my throat. Dear, dear Chelsea. What she'd gone through! How could I help her now?

"You said something today that was absolutely correct," I added, remembering our conversation on the bus. "About my obsession for poetry. Well, I looked up some verses in the Bible on the word *answer*, and guess what? I found a bunch of truly terrific Psalms."

"Why that word?"

"Remember how we were talking about echoes—from that poem by Longfellow?"

"Yeah?"

"Well, I decided to check out some verses using a similar word. And 'answer' was it."

"The book of Psalms does seem a little like poetry," she remarked.

"You're right."

Soon, we were talking about her worries and fears over her absentee mother. "Sometimes I get the feeling she doesn't love me anymore," Chelsea said.

"You're her own flesh and blood—the only child she's ever had. Of course she loves you."

I heard her sigh. "I wish none of this had ever happened, Merry. I really do!" She paused for a moment. "Will you read one of those verses you found?" she asked unexpectedly.

"Sure." I reached for my Bible. "Here's Psalm ninety-one, verse fifteen. It goes like this: 'He will call upon me, and I will answer him; I will be with him in trouble, I will deliver him and honor him.' "

"Wow," she whispered. "That 'he' in the verse could be anyone, right?"

"Yep."

She paused, then said, "Knowing that makes me feel a whole lot better."

"It's a comfort," I admitted. "We can count on those words, you know."

"Hey, I'm gonna look it up in our big, old family Bible."

"Good idea," I said.

It was getting late by the time we said our good-byes. And I was anxious to sleep away my headache; praying, too, that an end was soon to come to Chelsea's family nightmare.

SEVEN

Almost two weeks later, the lump on my head was completely gone. And—oh glory—the last day of school before Christmas break! It was also the day Levi Zook was scheduled to arrive home.

Getting off the bus after school, I glanced around almost sheepishly. In the distance, beyond the long grove of willow trees between my house and the Zooks' farm, I surveyed the area for clues of Levi's return.

"What's with you?" Chelsea cast a sideways stare.

I shrugged, not wanting to let on how nervous I was. She laughed. "Levi's nowhere in sight. Honest, Mer."

I said nothing and scurried toward the white-columned front porch. Chelsea and I headed inside by way of the front door—the quickest way to warmth. Smells of hot cocoa, mingled with freshly baked chocolate chip cookies, greeted us.

I hung up my coat, scarf, and gloves in the hall closet. "In case you didn't know it, my mom's a genius in the kitchen," I told Chelsea.

"You don't have to convince me." She yanked off her

snow boots and tossed her jacket onto the coatrack. Then the two of us, as if pulled by a magnet, hurried to the kitchen.

My mom, being the hostess she is, sat us down and brought steaming hot cocoa and a plateful of cookies to the table. "Did you girls have a good last day of school for the year?"

"Hey, that's right!" Chelsea said.

"No school till after New Year's, right?" I chimed in.

"Two incredible weeks away from school!" Gleefully, my friend reached for a cookie.

"Be sure to take some cookies home with you." Mom removed the red-and-green plaid apron she'd been wearing.

My friend's face seemed to radiate with the offer. "Thanks, Mrs. Hanson. My dad absolutely adores chocolate chip cookies. In fact, my mom used to make . . ." Her voice trailed off, and I felt a lump push up in my throat.

But leave it to my mother—a true master at steering conversation in a happier direction. And she certainly did that, maneuvering it clear away from Chelsea and right over to me. "Oh, Merry, you'll never guess who I saw today." There was mischief in her smile.

"Let me guess," I said, wrinkling my face. "Levi Zook?"

Mom blew lightly on her hot drink, then looked back at me. "Merry? What's the matter?"

"Nothing, really." Quickly, I got up to check on my

cats. They seemed to be having a heyday with their own milky snack.

My abrupt reaction may have been a bit too obvious—giving myself away. But I certainly did not want to discuss Levi. At least not in front of both my mom *and* my girlfriend.

Chelsea shot me a sympathetic look, and I leaned over to pet my furry friends, calling each one by name.

❧   ❧

Later, Chelsea and I were secluded away in my room. "Are you upset?" she probed.

"Not really."

"Does your mom know about Levi's letters?"

"She's not dense. And it *was* obvious that his letters were coming less often, if that's what you mean. But as far as ever reading them, no, Mom really doesn't know what he writes to me."

Chelsea sat on the floor and leaned back on the side of my bed. "What would she think if she knew he was in love with you?"

I laughed it off. "Levi's too young to know that."

"Meaning?"

"C'mon, you know what I'm saying." I joined her on the floor, sitting cross-legged, too. "After all the years growing up Amish, Levi's only now having a chance to experience the outside, modern world."

"So?"

I sighed. Why was she making me spell this out? "So I guess I really don't know how I feel about him anymore." There, I'd said it. Straight and clear.

"Aw, Mer, you've gotta be kidding me" was her reply. "You gave up a chance with Jon Klein last summer so you could hang out with Levi Zook. Now you're telling me you don't care about Levi?"

The confusion in her eyes was evident. My friend just didn't get it. But the longer we sat there, the more I realized that if I were to be honest with myself, I'd have to admit I didn't quite understand it, either.

Only time would tell. And, unfortunately, time was against me. Tomorrow was the skating party on Zooks' pond. Rachel had talked of nothing else for the past few days. Among other things, the party was to be an opportunity for me to meet Matthew Yoder, the boy who'd been taking her home from Saturday night singings for several months now. The boy she was sure would shine his flashlight onto her bedroom window someday—a time-honored signal among the Old Order Amish, indicating a marriage proposal.

"Echoes . . . only echoes of the past," I said. "That's all Levi and I have now."

She waved my comment into the air. "Merry, when will you ever come down out of that cloud of yours?"

I bobbed my head, looking around, pretending to see what she was talking about. "Hey, something *is* missing," I teased. "We need some music in here. How about some cloud music?"

She laughed but seemed to agree. So I turned on the radio and found my favorite contemporary Christian station. Maybe the music would drown out our conversation. Just in case there were curious ears nearby.

Then I had a flash of an idea. "I think it's high time for a photo update," I said, heading for my walk-in closet. "When was the last time you had your picture taken?"

She grinned. "September, for school pictures."

"That's much too long ago," I said, removing my best camera from its case. "It's nearly Christmas. Let's have a photo shoot and send some pics to your mom. Okay with you?"

Her face turned serious for a moment, then brightened. "Hey, maybe this is the answer—the very thing to entice my mom to hurry and get better."

I took off the lens cap and stopped in my tracks. "Wait a minute. Are you saying she doesn't have any pictures of you?"

"Nothing from the present, only the past." Her words came out sounding choked and dry.

"Maybe your *future* will rest on this." I motioned for her to lift her head a bit. "I'll take a roll of film, get it developed right away, and you can send the pictures off to her."

Click.

"And she'll have them before Christmas." She sighed audibly. "Only thing is, I wish Mom would come home to SummerHill instead."

"How about this," I continued. "Can you smile real big—you know, kinda make your eyes plead into the camera? Good. Now hold that pose right there."

Click.

Another nice shot. Chelsea was actually getting into the spirit of things.

In the end, I had what I thought might be seven or eight truly great poses. Out of a roll of twelve—not bad.

"Okay, first thing tomorrow, I'll have my dad take this roll to the one-hour film place."

"Great, Mer. Thanks."

I heard the camera do an automatic rewind, then took out the film and returned the camera to its leather case. "You might be able to mail the pictures to your mom by the time the postman comes tomorrow afternoon."

My plan seemed to please her, and she wore her happy face awhile longer.

When Mr. Davis stopped by for her around suppertime, Chelsea was loaded down with two boxes of home-baked goodies. "Thanks for everything," she called to Mom and me.

"Anytime." Mom waved to her.

We stood in the doorway, watching them pull away. I was delighted for having thought of the photo shoot. Chelsea had seemed almost cheerful when she left.

And I was thankful, too, for Mom's mouth-watering cookies, which had seemingly worked a healing all their own.

EIGHT

Just as I figured, the hours before the pond party were stressful ones. Honestly, I have to admit, I kept thinking Levi might show up on my back doorstep—plumb out of the blue—wanting to see me. But remarkably, and much to my relief, he didn't come.

I couldn't begin to count the times I went rushing down the hall to Skip's bedroom, though, to gaze out the window. Once, I even caught a glimpse of Levi hitching old Apple to the family carriage, probably so his mother could ride to one of the many quilting frolics going on this time of year. Seeing Levi from this distance, I felt nothing at all. No heart-pumping surges . . . nothing.

I knew I wouldn't be able to keep barging into Skip's room once he arrived home for the holidays, so I took every advantage to do so this morning.

Then it happened. While leaning on the windowsill and gazing in the direction of Zooks' farm, Mom strolled into the room.

Hearing her, I spun around. "Oh . . . hi, Mom."

"Merry?" She eyed me suspiciously. "What are you doing?"

"Oh, nothing really." And with that, I dashed from the room, feeling really silly. Embarrassed, too.

My mother had caught me gawking at the farmhouse next door. She was probably thinking that I simply couldn't wait to meet Levi for the skating party. Mom was smart about undeclared things like this. Really smart.

❧   ❧

Sunlight glinted off the snowy surface of fields and pastureland, creating a dazzling brightness as I walked the plowed road to the Zooks' later in the afternoon.

Old Man Winter had parceled out plenty of ice and snow—continually sending it our way—from the first weekend in December until now. In fact, in some peculiar way, it almost seemed as though the frigid temperatures and foul weather were somehow related to the arrival of Levi's last letter—the one saying he was coming home.

Anyway, I was dressed for the occasion: earmuffs, fur-lined gloves, long johns under my jeans, and my down-filled jacket. As I turned onto Zooks' private drive, I saw in the distance Levi, Rachel, and Matthew Yoder heading for the pond, their skates slung over their shoulders.

It almost startled me, how shy I felt. I even thought of turning back and going home. Why hadn't they waited for me? Was I late?

Over a week ago, Rachel had mentioned something about Levi coming to my house to pick me up for the occasion. It had sounded too much like a date, though, and

I had been determined that he not do such a thing. "Levi and I are really just good friends," I'd reminded her.

And Rachel must've remembered—most likely the reason the three of them were now approaching the wide pond ahead of me, and I was clear back here. By myself.

Nearing the farmhouse, I glanced at the window and spied Rachel's mother working in the kitchen. The dark green window shades had been pulled up all the way, making it easy for me to see inside. Nancy and Ella Mae flitted about, helping their mother bake bread and probably some spice cookies—Levi's favorite.

Big brother had returned. The prodigal had come home for Christmas. But it wasn't as if Levi were returning to the Amish church; he'd never joined, which, in many ways, was a good thing for him. Especially since he'd up and left the Amish community of SummerHill. Old Order Amish church members put their wayward members through a strict excommunication and shunning practice if they ever took a step away from their baptismal vow.

I kept going, following the barnyard and on over into the snowy meadow, stepping in the deep boot prints already made by the threesome ahead of me. The wintry path would lead me to the pond, which spanned half the width of Zooks' property and a portion of ours, as well.

Sections of the pond, especially out toward the east, were known to have deep, almost bottomless holes. All us kids knew about them because in the summer we loved to go diving in those spots. Sometimes, we'd even found treasures in the pond's "cellar," as we called the deepest places.

I heard a sound behind me and thought it was Aaron, the youngest Zook boy. Turning, I investigated.

"Merry, wait up!" the voice called.

When I stopped and really looked, I saw that Jon Klein was running toward me!

What on earth is he doing here? I wondered.

I waited while he caught up, and in my mind I pretended he was running in slow motion, only it was springtime and the daisies were a sea of yellow as he called my name.

"Hi, Jon," I said, bringing my short-lived fantasy to a close.

He stopped to catch his breath, and it was then that I noticed the gold flecks in his brown eyes. "Surprised to see silent me?"

"Silent?"

He nodded. "I've been following you since you made the turn into your neighbors' yard."

"Really?" I asked, surprised that I hadn't heard him before.

He pointed toward my house on the other side of the willow grove, just up the hill. "I doubt you can see it, but my dad's Jeep is parked in your yard. He came out to talk to your dad about something. Said I could come along and keep him company."

He was using alliteration to beat the band. And without thinking, it seemed.

Meanwhile, my heart had sped up. I was caught between ecstasy at Jon being here and worry—over how to involve him in Rachel's private pond party.

I certainly wouldn't be rude and send him away. Not Jon Klein, the guy I'd secretly had my eye on for as long as I could remember.

But what could I do? Invite him to go skating with us? What would Rachel say if I spoiled her "couples" event? And Levi? How would *he* react to Jon?

"Looks like you've got some plans," Jon said, offering to carry my skates.

"Uh . . . yeah." I relinquished my skates, thrilled at his thoughtful gesture. "A group of us from around here are going skating on Zooks' pond." I pointed to it, struggling with how to tell him that Levi Zook was one of the group.

"Sounds great. Mind if I watch?" he said.

"Me . . . mind?"

He laughed his warm, deep laugh, and we made our way through the snow together. "Wanna work the word game?" he asked.

Of course, I was dying to, but I glanced toward the pond, where the others were already beginning to lace up. "Maybe later," I said.

Something sank in me, and I felt helpless. Torn in half, in a strange sort of way.

Without warning, Jon stopped walking. "Listen, I really don't have to hang around here," he said quickly.

"No . . . no, I didn't mean you should go. Nothing like that." Truth was, I wanted him to stay. More than anything in the world!

He stood there, looking down at me with his inquisitive eyes. Little streams of breath floated around his mouth and nose. "I don't wanna intrude."

"Don't worry, Jon, you're not," I insisted. "C'mon!"

Running ahead, I felt the exhilaration. Jon was here—he was right here with me! The thought spurred me on, and I actually outran him.

"Merry, hullo!" Rachel called from the ice. She sped over to Jon and me. "I want ya to meet Matthew."

The stocky teenage Amish boy skated over and stuck out his hand. "Gut to know ya, Merry." He smiled broadly, showing his teeth. "Rachel here, she's been talkin' a lot about ya."

"Well, it's nice to meet you, too," I said, conscious that Levi was observing me as he glided across the pond toward us. Politely, I turned to Jon. "This is Jonathan Klein, a friend of mine from school." Then I introduced my Plain friends by their first names.

Before I could explain the reason why Jon was here, he spoke up. "My father's over visiting Merry's dad." He glanced at me almost shyly. "Merry had no idea I was coming."

Levi grinned at us. "Well, s'good to see ya again, Jonathan," he said. Then he looked straight at me. "How are *you*, Merry?"

"Fine, thanks. Are you glad to be home?" I replied, feeling worse than awkward.

Levi nodded. "I'd forgotten how much I missed this old place." Then looking out over the expanse of pond and meadow, he added, "I do believe there's plenty of room for the five of us. That is if Jonathan wants to slide around on the ice in his shoes."

We laughed, and then it hit me. Levi had remembered meeting Jon last summer. A short encounter, for sure, but another uncomfortable meeting—just outside the mall entrance in Lancaster.

"Uh . . . I don't have to skate, really," Jon offered.

But Matthew Yoder came to the rescue. "How 'bout if ya wear mine after bit?"

Rachel clapped her hands. "Oh, that's a wonderful-gut solution. You fellows'll take turns."

And that's what Matthew and Jonathan did—took turns. Someone else took turns, too.

Levi. He had to share his skating partner with the Alliteration Wizard. Although it didn't seem to bother Jonathan much, I saw the initial disappointment in Levi's eyes.

Still, we played everything from Fox and Geese to Crack the Whip. After an hour or more, Levi and Matthew built a bonfire on the south bank and we began to warm ourselves.

While we did, Rachel tried her best to teach Jon and me how to sing "What a Friend We Have in Jesus" in German. We did pretty well, I suppose, considering that neither of us had ever studied the language.

Jon seemed to be enjoying himself. And to be truthful, that was really all that mattered. At least to me.

After a time, Levi ran to the house and brought back a bag of marshmallows. While we toasted the gooey treats, we listened as he told of his church-building experiences in Bolivia. Matthew entered into the conversation, telling about his new workplace—the carpentry shop he now shared with his father. Rachel listened silently, eyes shining.

I remembered to tell Levi and Jon about Chelsea's interest in spiritual things. "She's been going to church with me lately," I said. "I hope you'll keep her in your prayers."

"We sure will," Levi said, offering me another marshmallow.

"Is her mom doing any better?" Jon asked.

"Chelsea and her dad are hoping she'll be home soon. Maybe in time for Christmas."

When Matthew asked about Jon's interests, the Alliteration Wizard said he enjoyed books. "Lots of them." He smiled at me. "Sometimes I even read poetry."

Poetry? Had he ever told me this? It was one more thing Jon and I had in common!

In a short while, we were all back on the ice. Except Matthew. He handed over his skates to Jon and kept the bonfire going as we played another round of Crack the Whip.

"Who wants to be the tail this time?" Rachel asked, grinning at me.

"Okay, I guess I will," I volunteered. "But only if you don't go too fast."

"Aw, the faster the better," Matthew called from the pond side, laughing heartily.

I shrugged. "Maybe for you."

Joking around, the four of us joined hands. Levi at the

center, followed by Rachel, then Jonathan. I was at the end. The tail.

Soon we were zooming around and around. Faster and faster, speeding across the ice in a giant circle. A group of jubilant young people, enjoying a sunny winter day.

Suddenly, quite unexpectedly, Jonathan stumbled over his skate. My grip broke free from his gloved hand as he tumbled forward.

I was airborne, flying across the pond's glassy surface. An outline of bare trees against the sky jeered at me in the distance.

I heard myself scream. "Help!"

Rachel was shouting at the top of her lungs. "Ach, Merry, no! There's thin ice!"

Hers were the last words I heard. The final sound was a terrifying *crack* as I plunged through the frozen surface—into the icy black hole below.

NINE

Numbing cold . . . raw, biting cold rushed in on all sides. My body responded with violent spasms. I'd fallen into liquid ice. This deep, deep hole . . . was sucking me down.

Call upon me, and I will answer. . . .

I attempted to touch bottom with my feet, still aware of my figure skates tied tightly around my ankles. But in spite of repeated efforts to find the depth, it was no use— the pond bed gave way to nothingness. I'd fallen into the "cellar."

Holding my breath, I tried to swim back to the opening above. Grappling with my hands and arms, I searched.

Where is it?

I made several attempts, aware that if I succumbed to having to see my way back and opened my eyes, they might freeze in their sockets. I grasped for something . . . anything to pull me up.

The pond mumbled in my ears, mocking me. Desperately, I thrashed about, my lungs aching for air.

Then as I fought to find the surface, my head bumped against something hard. I pushed on it, daring to open one eye.

Light burst all around me. I'd hit the pond's surface!

In one last frantic struggle, I pounded on the icy ceiling above me, praying. *Dear Lord Jesus, please help me!*

Ears throbbing, I broke through the opening, pulling hard for life-giving air, only to be pushed back into the frigid water by an unexpected, boy-sized body. Someone was trying to rescue me. . . .

But the chasm beneath wrenched at me, inhaling me. Down, down the pond's cellar tugged, slowly burying me in the arctic abyss. I was lost again. And in my stony confusion, something told me that one of two things was going to happen. I would either freeze to death . . . or drown. Die. Four days before Christmas.

Was this how it had been for Levi at age eleven? Had he sensed how close he was to drowning in this very pond, even as he struggled to yank his foot away from the willow root?

I had saved him that day six years ago. Saved him. . . .

Who would save *me*?

Precious seconds ticked by, merging with the frozen underwater blackness. My lungs screamed for breath; my body stiffened, paralyzed.

An eternity later—surreal and unexpected—a tiny, yet hazy form began to emerge out of the murky darkness. When I looked more closely, I knew that it was Faithie, my little twin, swimming toward me.

It did not occur to me to question how or why my

dear, dead sister was here with me now. Yet I could feel her loving arms encircle me, guiding me. "You must not breathe yet, Merry," she warned. "Wait . . . wait. . . ."

❧   ❧

The heaviness in my chest was the first sensation I felt when I regained consciousness. Slowly, painstakingly, I forced the sounds and smells of this new place to separate themselves in my mind.

Then my mother's face, distorted and wavy, began to sharpen a bit—coming into focus. "Is this heaven?" I asked. "Did I die?"

"No, darling, you're very much alive." She squeezed my hand.

If I was alive, why did I feel so dead?

Within seconds, I felt my body yielding to sleep again. But in my drifting, I felt my mother's hand still holding mine, and a thousand questions faded away.

❧   ❧

The next face I recognized was Daddy's. A whole twenty-four hours later, one of the nurses remarked. He looked downright exhausted, probably because he'd gone without sleep for a very long time.

"It hurts to breathe," I told him.

"Try not to talk, honey bunch," he said as another doctor examined me.

I didn't feel up to talking. Especially later when several strangers came in to visit. Two boys and a girl.

Levi and Jonathan were the boys' names. The girl was

very sweet—someone by the name of Rachel. She said she was Levi's sister and cried when I didn't remember them.

All of this seemed very confusing. Why were they so happy to see me when I didn't even know who they were?

When I asked my mom about it later, her face turned pale. And hours later, in the privacy of my hospital room, she and Dad told me that I'd lost certain portions of my memory.

"Is it serious?" I asked. "Will my memory come back?"

Dad smiled slightly, stroking my hair. "You had a horrible accident. We almost lost you, baby." And he began to explain what had happened Saturday afternoon on the pond.

"Why can't I remember?" I put my hand to my forehead, trying to think, but it only made my head hurt worse. "Who did you say rescued me?"

He sighed. "Well, your friend from school, Jonathan Klein, literally jumped into the pond, trying to bring you up to the surface for air."

Mom chimed in. "But you sank back down, and he couldn't find you."

"Which pond?" I asked.

"Our Amish neighbors'—out behind our property and the Zooks'."

"Zooks?" The name sounded foreign to me, but Mom and Dad were talking as though these people—the Zooks—were long-time friends.

"Tell her what happened next," Mom prompted Dad.

A smile burst across his face. "Your childhood friend,

Levi Zook, risked his life to save both you and Jon."

"Levi?"

"He's the one who saved you and your school friend," Dad explained.

"Well, whoever these boys are, I want to thank them— both of them. Levi . . . and Jim?"

"*Jon*," Mom said. "Short for Jonathan."

The nurse came in to take my blood pressure, and while she did, she asked if I remembered her name. I fooled her and read it off her name badge. But she patted my arm as though I'd said the wrong thing, then left.

When my brother came in, my parents started introducing him. "This is your big brother, Skip," my dad said. "He's home from his freshman year in college—for Christmas."

"You don't have to tell me who my own brother is," I said, which made Skip and everyone smile. "So when's Christmas?" I asked.

"In three days," Mom said, glancing away. She took a tissue out of her purse and dabbed at her eyes. And I had an empty feeling. Something was terribly wrong.

That is, until Chelsea Davis, my spunky girlfriend, showed up and I recognized her, too. "Hey, Mer, whatcha doin' in the hospital? It's almost Christmas, for Pete's sake!"

Mom assured me that Chelsea had already heard about my skating accident. "But she's curious to know what happened to the pictures you took of her. She was going to send them to her mother."

"Oh yeah," I said, remembering. "Ask Dad . . . he

was supposed to have them developed. I forget the exact day, though."

My parents and Skip—Chelsea, too—started clapping. "Way to go, Merry," my redheaded friend declared.

"Come here, you." I motioned to her. "Is your mom better?"

"About the same."

"So you've heard from her again?"

"Just a few minutes on the phone."

"But you'll be able to get the pictures to her, won't you?" I asked. "In time for Christmas?"

Chelsea nodded, glancing at my dad. He gave us a thumbs-up gesture. "Don't worry about a thing," she said. "I'm planning to deliver them to Mom in person. Daddy and I are going for a surprise visit."

"When?"

Her eyes shone. "Christmas Eve."

"But I thought—"

"No, Mom won't be home for Christmas this year," she interrupted. "It's just not the right time for her, I guess."

"I'm sorry, Chels."

"Me too, but hey, it's better than nothing, right?"

We talked awhile longer—about the recent snow storm (one I'd missed while cooped up at Lancaster General), as well as Chelsea's Christmas list. "Mom's homecoming is at the top of my list," she said.

"I don't blame you. It's the best wish of all." I started to cough.

Almost on cue, the therapist came in and massaged

my lungs—front and back. When she was gone, I wiggled my finger, indicating that I wanted Chelsea to lean over so I could whisper something. "That guy—the one who pulled me out of the pond—do you think he's cute?"

She chuckled. "Levi's a college man," she whispered back to me, "studying to be a minister or missionary. He's older."

"How old?"

"Seventeen, I think."

I decided right then and there—I didn't care what she said, this Levi fellow sounded pretty good to me. A real hero, too!

"But," she added, "the other guy, the one who jumped into the pond after you, now *he's* the one you always liked best, even though he's a bit of a bookworm."

"Jim?"

"Jon, short for Jonathan. Remember?"

"Not really, but what a nice name."

She shrugged. "Nice enough, I guess."

Her answer made me curious. Who *was* this Jon fellow, and why did I like him so much?

TEN

The college boy, the one studying to be a minister, came for a visit with his sister the next morning. She was wearing a long green dress with a black apron and a white head covering. I wondered where she'd gotten such an unusual outfit, but I was polite not to ask.

"Hullo, Merry," Levi said, hovering near the hospital bed. "Rachel and I have been worried about ya."

"Worried?" I said.

Rachel spoke up softly. "Because you don't remember who we are. It's not like ya at all." She looked down at me with gentle eyes. "You're our dear friend, Merry. And our cousin, too."

I glanced at Levi, feeling suddenly strange about having asked Chelsea if he was cute. "We're related?"

"Jah, but only in a distant way," Rachel said, her dimples showing.

"I'm very sorry that I don't know you . . . er, remember you," I volunteered quickly, "but hopefully, my memory will return soon. For now, though, I want to say thank you, Levi, for saving my life."

"The way I see it," he replied, "I do believe it was the right and gut thing to do, savin' ya thata way, Merry."

I studied his short brown hair and blue eyes. He was tall and lanky—quite handsome, really. And there was such a kindhearted way about him.

"You see," he continued, "back when you and I were youngsters, you saved *me* from drownin' once."

"I did?"

How very strange that I could've saved him, I thought. *Aren't I much younger than Levi Zook?*

He nodded, a twinkle in his eye. "Jah, Merry. You did."

The soft, gentle way he said my name made me want to get well instantly. Maybe then I'd have a chance at getting better acquainted with this soft-spoken boy.

"Well, I really wish I could remember that day," I said, studying his sister.

Rachel, eyes cast down, went to sit by the window, leaving Levi and me somewhat alone in the room. I was a bit surprised when her brother touched my hand. He held it lightly as he told me about the summer I was nearly nine and he was eleven. "We'd all gone swimmin' in the pond out behind the barn—same one where ya fell through the ice. Anyways, we kept on divin' into them 'cellar' holes out over near the east side of the pond. And wouldn'tcha know it, my big brother, Curly John, pulled himself up a scrap piece of metal deep down."

"Did you say a cellar . . . in the pond?" I was thoroughly confused—remembering only some of what he'd said.

Smiling, Levi showed his teeth. "That's what we always called the deepest part," he explained.

A flicker of a memory danced in my mind, then faded. "Oh," I said, catching my breath.

He leaned over, gazing down at me. "Merry, are ya all right?"

"I think so . . . it was . . . just something I thought I was about to remember."

With that comment, Rachel rushed over, and Levi let go of my hand. "What was my brother just now sayin' to ya? Somethin' about the cellar hole out there in the pond?"

"Jah, that's right." Levi nodded, filling her in. "Do ya remember the summer Curly John found himself a souvenir from the bottom of the pond?"

"Ach, sure do," she said.

"Well, I wasn't gonna be outdone, so I dove in head-first," Levi continued. "As far down as I could go without drowning, I went, searchin' all over for something to bring back up."

"And 'pride goeth before a fall'—ain't it so?" Rachel teased. "You went and got yer foot caught in that willow root and near drowned."

"Sure would've, if it hadn't been for Merry here." He looked at me with dancing eyes. And for one silly minute, I thought I might be falling in love.

❧　　❧

Chelsea came for a visit about an hour after Rachel and Levi left. She brought the pictures I'd taken of her posing in my room. "They're really good," she said. "Wanted you to see how they turned out."

I'd always been very critical of my work, so I studied each of the twelve pictures carefully. Even though Chelsea thought they were good, only six of the shots were tops in my opinion.

She handed me two five-dollar bills. "This'll help pay for the film and processing."

"Oh, keep your money, really."

"But I want to give you something." Chelsea plopped the money down on the table beside my bed. "You can't imagine how glad my mom'll be to get these."

"She'll probably be happier to see *you* in person," I quipped. "How long has it been?"

"She left on October third, over two and a half months ago."

I was wheezing heavily now and propped myself up with more pillows. "I'll keep praying for you and your dad. For your mom, too."

"Thanks." She pulled up a chair. "Hey, has Jon Klein come to see you again?"

"I'm not really sure," I said. "You could ask my mom, though. There were several visitors here when I was out of it the first couple days."

"You were zonked, all right. But you're doing better, aren't you, Mer?"

I smiled back at her. "The docs are saying I might get to go home for Christmas Eve. That is if I promise to take my antibiotics and let Mom give me my lung massages."

"Hey, cool. That's tomorrow."

We chitchatted some more, but Chelsea seemed most interested in discussing Jonathan Klein—the boy who'd so bravely jumped into the icy pond water, attempting to save me. Or so my father had told me.

"Mind if I give you a little background on this guy?" She reached into her jacket pocket and pulled out a folded paper. "I found this in your desk drawer . . . at your house. But don't freak out, your mom gave me permission, okay?"

I leaned forward to see. "What is it?"

"It's a note—from Jon Klein, the boy you really like. But since you're in a fog zone right now, you'll just have to trust me, Mer. Anyway, he passed this note to you in math class. You may not remember, but he did. Honest. You told me yourself." She handed the note to me. "Take a look."

I began to read it—very unusual the way each sentence was constructed around a single letter of the alphabet. "This is some weird writing."

She agreed. "That's what I thought last week when I first read it. But the thing I can't let you overlook is that you . . . *you* are crazy about this guy, Mer. Before you nearly drowned, you and he would always meet everyday at school at—"

A faint image sprang up. "At our lockers?"

"Hey, that's right! What else?"

I sank back onto my pillows. The impression had fizzled. "I don't know now. It's gone."

"Tell me . . . what did you remember just now?"

I stared at the many get-well baskets and vases of

flowers lining the shelf along the windowsill, thinking back to the past few seconds. I tried squeezing the recollection out of my brain, forcing it into my consciousness. "Something about lockers at school. I could almost see my combination lock dangling."

Chelsea was hopping happy. "This is truly terrific."

"Hey, isn't 'truly' *my* word?" I said, laughing now. Laughing so hard, I began to cough.

For some reason, she ran out of the room, bringing my mom back with her. "I think it's happening," Chelsea exclaimed. "I think her memory's kicking in!"

❧   ❧

Jon Klein was my very last visitor of the day. "Finally," he said, "I timed things to a tee."

"Was I sleeping when you came before?"

He nodded. "Snoozing so soundly, very still, silent . . . such sleep."

"Oh . . ." Another image shot past. "What's that you're doing? All the *s*'s?"

He grinned, standing tall next to my hospital bed. "It's our word game, Merry, Mistress of Mirth. Can you still talk alliteration-eze?"

I shrugged. "Whatever *that* is."

He began to explain, stopping to run his hand through his hair. He seemed a bit frustrated. "C'mon, Mistress Merry. Think through it."

I shook my head. "I have no idea what you're talking about—a word game? And what's with the nickname?"

His face drooped at my response.

"Look, I'm real sorry," I said, "but I don't know what to say about the strange language you speak."

"Hey, you're doing it." His face brightened. "You're starting to alliterate!"

"I am? What do you mean, Jim?"

He looked hurt just then, and I wondered if I'd forgotten something. Like maybe calling him the wrong name.

Again.

ELEVEN

I was thrilled when the doctor said I'd be going home for sure. Being stuck in the hospital at Christmastime was anything but fun!

Our one-hundred-year-old farmhouse had never looked so good as it did when I first spied it from a quarter-mile away. The idyllic words from Longfellow's "Song" boosted my spirits.

> *Stay, stay at home, my heart, and rest;*
> *Home-keeping hearts are happiest,*
> *For those that wander they know not where*
> *Are full of trouble and full of care;*
> *To stay at home is best.*

My white figure skates were lying on the floor near the radiator in my room when I arrived. Honestly, they felt like soaked cardboard—coerced to dry out. There they were, greeting me home, ugly as all get out. I decided I never wanted to wear them again. In fact, I didn't even want to look at them. So when Mom came upstairs to serve some sort of soup, I asked her to throw them away.

"Something bothering you, honey?" She eyed me curiously.

"It's the skates. I don't like looking at them. They remind me of . . ." I didn't know for sure.

She didn't argue, just put them in an old shoe box and closed my closet door. "How's that? Out of sight, out of mind."

"Much better."

She came over and felt my forehead. "I'm so glad to have you back home. We all are."

"Me too. I hate hospitals. They're a hassle. Home's a haven, a much happier place."

Mom looked at me funny. "Merry, why are you talking that way?"

"What way?"

"Everything's . . . uh, kind of alliterated."

"It is?"

She scratched her head and smiled. "You know, there are some people who would love to be able to do that naturally."

"Jim?"

"Who?"

"The boy who tried to save me but fell in the pond instead?"

"Oh, you mean Jon . . . Jonathan Klein?" She frowned a little. "Why? Does *he* talk that way?"

"He did at the hospital yesterday."

Mom paused to make a fuss over my cats, who were

beginning to crowd me on my bed. Then she left the room.

Why did I keep forgetting this guy's name? And what on earth had been so wonderful about him? I struggled to remember who he was—and what it was that he and I liked to do at our lockers every day.

Was Chelsea just giving me a hard time? Why would I go gaga over a guy with a hang-up for head rhyme?

Deciding to get to the bottom of this, I pulled out my eighth-grade yearbook from last year. Then, so Mom wouldn't worry that I'd have a setback, I slipped back into bed and began to browse.

There were plenty of pictures of Jon Klein—no sports shots, though. Jon was on student council and did all kinds of other academic type stuff. And from the looks of things, he was super smart. Even made the honor roll both semesters!

I closed the book and let my cats creep closer to me on my comforter. What had attracted me to Jon Klein anyway? Besides being a Christian and well-groomed, what else did we have in common?

Chelsea might know, I decided. When she called to tell me about her Christmas Eve visit with her mother, I'd ask her more about Jon.

I must admit, I could hardly wait.

Dad arrived home earlier than usual from his duties at the ER. He came right upstairs to see me. "How's my girl doing?" He kissed me on the top of my head and sat on the edge of my bed.

"I'm feeling better, I think. Ready to tackle the Christmas tree—what's *under* the tree, that is."

He smiled, looking far less tired than he had earlier in the week. "Would you like to go downstairs? There's a rip-roaring fire in the fireplace. It's the place to be on Christmas Eve."

"I'll do anything to get closer to the presents," I teased.

He scooped me up in his arms and carried me downstairs, planting me on the living room sofa in front of a crackling fire.

In the corner stood a nine-foot tree, showering the room with twinkling white light. The tree filled the expanse of space between the hardwood floor and the high ceiling—typical of the old Pennsylvania farmhouses. Mom had carefully trimmed its thick branches with clusters of cream-colored grapes, babies' breath, pearl hearts, dried hydrangeas, ivory angels, and snowy-white poinsettias. Definitely a white theme this year, and by the looks of so many winged messengers, an angelic one, too.

Soon Mom came running with afghans, and Skip brought cushions for my back. My family fluttered about me, plumping up pillows and making sure every inch of me was covered in warmth. Except my head, of course.

"Better watch it," I warned. "You'll have me spoiled in no time."

"Too late," Skip said, laughing.

Dad pulled up his easy chair closer to the sofa. "So,

tell me, did you remember anything new today?"

I stared at the tree. "Well, for no reason at all, I sorta remembered the deep snow on the day I nearly drowned. The wind, too."

He nodded. "We did have quite a lot of snow prior to your accident. And again afterward," he said softly. "Anything else?"

"Echoes. There were echoes in the wind. In my ears . . . I could hear whispering in my ears as I—yes, that's it, I remember skating now. I really do!"

"Who was with you, Merry?" Dad seemed terribly excited, leaning forward as he anticipated my answer.

I strained to recall. But not a single soul came to mind.

The phone jangled me out of my reverie, and a few minutes later, Mom appeared in the doorway. "Are you up to a phone call, Merry?"

"Who is it?"

"Lissa Vyner. She said it'll just be a minute."

"Sure, I'll talk to her."

Dad picked up the evening paper and began to read. I waited patiently for Mom to bring in the cordless phone. She came smiling, bringing it along with a cup of herbal tea for me. Carefully, she set the teacup and saucer on the coffee table. "The tea's very hot, so don't burn your tongue," she whispered as I took the phone from her.

"Hello?" I said.

"How *are* you, Merry?" My friend's voice cheered me immediately. "Everyone's been asking about you."

I wondered who *everyone* was. "Well, I'm home from the hospital, that's the best thing. That place tends to smell a little offensive, know what I mean?"

"The antiseptic, probably."

"Yeah, that and other icky stuff."

We talked about her grandmother, who she said was scheduled to arrive any minute. "Grammy Vyner's still bragging about the pictures you took of me in my junior bridesmaid's dress. On your porch last July . . . remember?"

"Of course I do. Just because I blocked out random chunks of my life doesn't mean I've gone completely senile."

"I didn't mean that, really." She apologized all over the place. "Oh, Merry, there's something I have to tell you before we hang up. It's about Jon Klein."

"What about him?"

"He called last night and started talking in some sort of bizarre code or something."

"What do you mean?"

"I'm not sure I can describe it. I guess you could call it alliteration, except doesn't that usually show up in poetry—stuff like that?"

"Other places, too. I've seen it in good literature."

"Is he into some new author or what?" she asked.

I glanced at Dad, whose head was bobbing while he tried to read the paper. I was determined not to snicker, but it was very hard to keep a straight face.

"Merry?" she said, calling me back to the conversation at hand.

"Oh, sorry, Liss, it's just that you should see my dad. He's trying to read the paper, and he keeps falling asleep."

She didn't seem to care what my father was doing at the moment. "I just thought maybe you could give me some idea about Jon's latest craze. That's all."

"Me?" I sighed. "I wish I could help you, but I have no idea who Jon Klein really is. Everyone keeps telling me how attached I was to him before. . . ." I stopped for a moment.

Lissa jumped in. "Oh, it's true, Merry. I think you really *did* like Jon Klein before you nearly drowned."

"But why was he skating with me that day? What was that all about?"

"Well, did you ever think that maybe Jon likes you?" she said. "Maybe *that's* why he was there."

An awkward silence fell between us, then she continued. "I really hope you have a great Christmas, and I'm so sorry about your accident. Who knows what horrible thing might've happened if Levi Zook hadn't saved you."

"He's a mighty special guy, that Levi. At least you can understand *him* when he talks," I joked.

We giggled a little, then hung up.

"Dad?" I whispered to my dozing parent, putting the phone on the coffee table. "It's almost suppertime."

He snorted awake, blinking his eyes. "Uh . . . sorry. What did I miss?"

"Oh, just some girl talk. Nothing earthshaking."

He sat up and straightened himself. "I don't think I mentioned this to you since your accident, but Jon

Klein's father came to see me on Saturday afternoon. That's why the boy was over at the Zooks' farm when you fell through the ice."

I listened, wondering what he was about to tell me.

"Seems that your friend is interested in photography—same as you. I gave his dad some pointers on what kind of camera and lens equipment to get. But it's supposed to be kept top-secret, so don't say anything."

"Jon wants a camera for Christmas?" It seemed that maybe Chelsea hadn't been pulling my leg after all. What was it she'd said? That I'd had a major crush on Jon Klein?

"Yesiree, Jonathan's getting a big surprise come tomorrow," Dad announced.

"So you're saying he's into photography?"

"Absolutely."

Just then Mom came to serve me a hearty bowl of homemade vegetable barley soup for my Christmas Eve supper. Dad got up and headed for the dining room, two rooms away. I could hear him getting settled at the elegant holiday table that Mom had no doubt set for the rest of the family. But it was their hearty laughter that caught me off guard, if only for a second.

The sounds of their chuckling reminded me of something. Something jovial. Laughter . . . on ice. Echoes of fun—all the wintry games. Echoes began to wing the events back to me.

Slowly they came, little by little. . . .

An Amish boy stood near a bonfire. He was calling to me. *The faster the better*, he said.

Those of us on the ice began to play a game of Crack the Whip. Faster and faster we flew.

Someone tripped and fell, breaking the chain of hands.

Then someone screamed. Who? Was it Rachel? Was it my own frightened screams?

With all my might, I tried to think what came next, wondering hard why Chelsea had insisted that I surely must've been delighted to be skating with Jon that day.

In spite of myself, no such information or emotion emerged from my scattered memory. It was as if someone had closed the door on it. Tight.

TWELVE

I was beginning to resent the constant questioning from my family. Chelsea and Lissa, too. Everyone seemed more interested in helping me remember than anything else. People were more concerned about my temporary loss of memory than they were about my upper-respiratory infection, which had come from swallowing icy pond water and being exposed to the raw elements.

All during that Christmas Day, I was barraged with one reminder after another that I'd forgotten a whopping twenty-four hours . . . and much more. Not to mention a few key people, too.

Levi Zook, however, had a totally different approach to things. He came with a gift for me Christmas afternoon, long after our family gift opening and a splendid dinner of prime rib and scrumptious trimmings.

I was resting in the living room, staring into the fire, trying my best to boost my brain.

"Merry, you have company," Mom said softly, showing Levi into the room and arranging the chairs so he and I could alternate looking at both the fireplace and the

Christmas tree. Not so much at each other.

Levi, slender and fit, seemed content to sit in Mom's big Boston rocker, holding the rectangular-shaped gift box in his lap. For the longest time, he sat very still, not allowing the chair to move. He looked very handsome in his light blue sweater. "How are ya feelin' today, Merry?" he asked in a whispery voice.

"Getting stronger every day, thanks."

He glanced down at the present in his hands. "I brought a little something for ya." Handing it to me, he beamed an innocent, yet charming, smile. "God bless ya, Merry. Happy Christmas."

"Thank you, Levi," I said, feeling a bit giddy.

I opened the gift—a box of assorted chocolates. "Enjoy the sweets when you're all well, jah?"

I assured him that I'd wait. "It was so nice of you to think of me."

He leaned toward me slightly. "Oh, Merry, I'm always thinking of ya. Always."

My heart skipped a beat, and I have to admit, I was a bit relieved when he turned to admire Mom's large antique nativity figurines displayed on the hearth.

"God's been so good," he was saying. "To think what might've happened out there on the pond. . . ."

"Let's not talk about that," I said.

Then he began to reminisce about our childhood days—riding in the Zooks' pony cart, pitching hay with the grown-ups, swinging on the rope in the hayloft, sampling his mother's jams and jellies.

Slowly, deliberately, he worked his way through the

years, to our teen years. "Last summer was a real special time for us, Merry," he remarked. "We even had a nice buggy ride in the rain one Sunday afternoon."

He didn't ask me if I remembered, but I listened anyway, telling my brain to relax for a change.

"Miss Spindler, our neighbor, raced right past us in her sports car. Ach, you were so worried that she'd spread it around SummerHill that you and I were seein' each other."

"And she did, too, didn't she?" I spoke up.

Levi grinned. "That's right! The busybody told your daddy that she'd seen us together. And you got the willies, thinkin' I'd be gettin' myself in trouble for taking a pretty 'English' girl for a ride in my open carriage."

I felt myself blush at his comment, remembering vaguely what he was talking about. But the more Levi spoke, the more I knew for sure that I liked him.

"How's your college study?" I asked, relying on the information Chelsea had given me.

"Well, to be honest with ya, it's the best thing I ever did for myself. So much of what I always wanted to do is happening now. The Lord's work is all around me, Merry. I'm excited about preachin' the Gospel—and very soon."

The joy in his heart was evident in his eyes. They sparkled as he spoke, matching the bright surroundings of tree and tinsel.

But something else was happening. Levi was behaving as if I'd never forgotten who he was. Or the carefree, romantic ties we'd once had together. Truly exciting.

Things were not as comfortable, though, between Jon Klein and me when he called a little bit later. "Merry Christmas, Merry, maiden of misery," he said, then laughed apologetically. "It's jovial Jon, or at least that's what you used to call me."

"Before I fell through thin ice?" I said, not sure he was joking.

He ignored my remark. "How was your holy holiday?"

"Okay, I guess." I noticed his use of *h*'s, but didn't say anything. My mind was on something else—wondering if I should inquire about the surprise present from his parents.

Before I could get the words out, he brought it up. "You'll never guess what my folks gave me for Christmas."

I didn't blurt out the answer in case he hadn't received the camera equipment yet. "I really hate guessing games," I said, still feeling strange talking to this guy who seemed to know me so well, in spite of myself.

"I'll give you a hint." Unfortunately, the hint he was talking about had much more to do with his eagerness for me to remember the past. And specifically, for me to recall who *he* was . . . and that ridiculous word game he kept referring to.

I resented his style of prompting my defunct gray matter. Couldn't he simply accept me as I was? The way Levi Zook did?

Jon kept talking, though, about my love of nature— my known desire to capture God's beauty on film. I had a funny feeling he was working up to telling me about the grand surprise he'd received from his parents.

"Hey, do you remember the cool shot you took behind Chelsea's house?" he asked.

"The one in the woods?"

"Right—the picture you entered in the annual school contest back in October."

I laughed. "You mean the one that placed second?"

"That's it." Then curiously, he began to backtrack, discussing in detail the area behind Chelsea's house—the lot near the isolated shanty.

"Look, Jon," I said at last, "you don't have to help me remember any of that. I haven't blocked out *everything*—only certain times . . . and people."

"So what's causing it—your memory loss?" He seemed restless about my condition. Not worried, but almost impatient.

"My dad says amnesia can occur for several reasons. One, the trauma of my accident. And even a slight concussion, which I had a couple of weeks ago, can bring it on, too."

"But it's only your short-term memory, right?" he probed.

"And some scattered memories—random memory, I guess you'd say."

"When will it all come back?" he asked.

His attitude frustrated me. "Do you have to be so antsy about this?"

"Aw, Merry, don't go getting all upset."

"Well, since you put it that way, I *am* angry. I mean,

all you've done since we got reacquainted, or whatever, is force me to remember you." I sighed. "You and that weird word game . . . well—"

"Hey, that's good, Merry. Keep going!"

I had no idea what on earth he was saying, but at this point in the conversation, I just wanted to bail out. "Thanks, Jon. It was nice of you to phone—but I've gotta get going."

He was whooping it up. "Merry, did you just hear yourself? You're doing it—you're alliterating!"

"I'm sorry," I said. "I don't know what you're talking about. Good-bye."

I didn't actually slam the phone down or even hang up on him, but it was definitely an abrupt farewell. Funny thing was, I felt no guilt for my actions. After all, I didn't really know him. Not anymore, at least.

Clicking the off button on the phone, I leaned back, taking in the dazzling decorations around me. Mom had outdone herself this year. Above each window dressing, white satin bows, crisscrossed with grapevines, served as folksy ornaments. Centered on the mantel, a spray of white long-stemmed tulips framed the broad fireplace. And an array of ivory candles—some round, others tall, all of differing heights—on both sides of the centerpiece created a truly ethereal effect.

Gazing at the flickering lights, I began to recall fragments of the bonfire at the ice skating party.

Levi had gone back to the house to get marshmallows, and we roasted them on the ends of coat hangers. It was one of those never-to-be-forgotten moments, full of nostalgia and wistful rememberings—something I'd want to tell my grandchildren about someday. Not so much because of the people involved. It had more to do with the setting, the tingly feeling of expectation in the air—the wintry delight that had pervaded the atmosphere around us.

Both Levi and Jon had offered to help me with the simple chore of poking my marshmallows through with a hanger wire, even though I was entirely capable of cooking up my own treat. That much of the significant day I *did* remember. I was surprised how easily it wafted back to me—to my present consciousness.

Now if only I could get a grasp of my relationships with both Levi and Jon. Especially Jon. It was the one thing that truly bugged me about this Christmas.

THIRTEEN

Miss Spindler, also known as Old Hawk Eyes—the neighbor lady who lived in the house behind ours (give or take half an acre)—breezed in for a visit late Christmas afternoon.

I was still hacking away, trying not to cough all over everyone, even though the doctors said I wasn't contagious. Mom, bless her heart, was still gently massaging my lungs at various intervals—doctor's orders. But I was up and about for short periods, had even sat at the table for Christmas dinner. According to my medical genius father, I was making solid progress.

Being cooped up in the house, no matter how beautifully decorated, was truly a pain for some people. I, being one of those prone to cabin fever, had to resort to other things for my entertainment. Things besides TV. I'd never been much of a television watcher, so I was actually delighted when I heard Miss Spindler's old voice crackle in our kitchen.

I sprang from my solitary post on the living room couch—surrounded by the new poetry and photography books Mom and Dad had given me for Christmas—and tiptoed toward the kitchen.

Miss Spindler had come bearing gifts: two pumpkin pies and three-dozen snickerdoodle cookies. "How's every little thing?" she asked when I peeked around the corner. Her blue-gray hair was done up in a bouffant style, and it looked as if she'd swept much of it from the lower section of her head to cover the meager patches at the crown.

Quickly, Mom spoke up on my behalf. "Merry's recovering quite nicely." She didn't go on to mention my memory lapses, though. Thank goodness.

Miss Spindler smiled at me, nodding her head. "I can see the dear girl's improving. Her smeller's a-workin', ain't it?"

I had to chuckle. Leave it to Old Hawk Eyes to make an on-the-spot assessment of my physical condition based on my response to a couple of spicy pumpkin pies.

Being careful not to go near our drafty back door, I pulled out a kitchen chair close to the radiator and sat down, enjoying the warmth as it drifted around me.

"Talk has it that our little darlin's suffering from amnesia these days," Miss Spindler continued.

I wondered how Mom would go about explaining things.

She began by setting down mugs of hot apple cider on the table for our guest, herself, and me. "Merry doesn't have full-blown amnesia. This type of traumatic memory loss can last anywhere from a few hours to several weeks."

Our nosy neighbor kept sending persistent glances my

way, but I remained absolutely quiet.

Mom gave me a reassuring smile. "We're doing everything the doctors said to do for our girl."

The way my mother put things sometimes gave me reason to smile. She was quite the lady, my mom. And here she was making semi-small talk with SummerHill's biggest gossip.

"Well, what on earth is causin' Merry's brain to fuzz up?" Miss Spindler asked, looking for all the world as though she was genuinely interested in my present mental state.

Mom took her time sipping the cider, then looked at me with a twinkle in her eye. "You may have heard about Merry's mishap on the ice last week?"

"Oh, dear me, yes indeedy, I did!" And there was probably no telling what sort of spin on the actual facts she'd heard and possibly reconcocted by now!

"Well, sometimes trauma can trigger a short-term memory loss," Mom replied. "But we're not worried about it, so please, Miss Spindler, don't you be, either."

The woman sighed and held her bony hand up to her chest. I could see her breathing heavily, up and down, like she was near ready for a fit or stroke or who knows what. Anyway, after a few minutes, Miss Spindler settled down and let my mom talk reason to her.

But the most interesting aspect of the discussion came as Old Hawk Eyes was about to say good-bye. "You do know, Merry, that one of your Amish friends—Levi Zook, I believe—is responsible for yer bein' alive this very minute."

I was surprised to hear this revelation from her lips.

"Yes, indeedy," she said. "That there Levi done pulled ya out, Merry—that other fella, too."

Mom's mouth actually dropped open. "How do you know all this?" she asked.

A curious expression snuck up on Miss Spindler's face, and suddenly she clammed up. It was as if she'd been caught telling on herself. "Oh, bless my soul, I guess I best be headin' home now." She glanced over her shoulder at the kitchen window. "Well, I'll be, lookee there. It's a-comin' down mighty good again. I tell ya, this is the most snow we's seen around here for many a winter."

Miss Spindler was right about that. The snows had come hard and lay good and heavy for most of December. Thing was, she wasn't about to fess up to any spying tactics or reveal whatever made it possible for her to see all the way to Zooks' pond and beyond.

Still, I couldn't help but push for some answers. From what she'd already said, I figured she'd secretly observed what happened on the ice from her attic window or somewhere else. "Any idea how Levi went about saving me, Miss Spindler?" I asked.

A smile passed over her face, and for an instant, she honestly looked like one of the angels on our Christmas tree. "Ever heard tell of a human rope?" she said softly.

"Are you saying Levi had some help?" I said.

Unexpectedly, Miss Spindler seemed more than eager to spill out her information, yet not willing to share the precise method for acquiring it. "Three other young people were there, all right. They got themselves right down on the ice—down close to the thinnest part—and I tell ya, they pulled on each other for dear life."

From the sound of this, it seemed that Old Hawk Eyes had witnessed my rescue—Jon Klein's, too!

"Thanks for telling me," I found myself saying. "You don't know how much it means to me, knowing this, Miss Spindler."

When she was ready to leave, the old woman got up and walked to the back door with Mom accompanying her. "Happy New Year, Mrs. Hanson, Missy Merry," Ruby Spindler said with a crooked smile.

"Oh, do be careful on the snow," Mom cautioned.

In the still of dusk, the crackly voice came back, "Oh, don'tcha be worryin' none."

Two of my cats, Shadrach and Meshach, raised their eyelids as a gust of cold wind blew through the kitchen.

"Can you imagine?" Mom said, shaking her head. "She saw it all happen . . . your accident. Somehow Miss Spindler saw you fall through the ice."

"It's truly amazing" was all I could say.

Mom's eyes were on the ceiling as if reliving the frightful day. "Well *that* explains how the paramedics arrived so quickly." She seemed a bit dazed. "Do you realize that Ruby Spindler may have played a role in saving your life, Merry?"

I appreciated Mom's sentiments toward Old Hawk Eyes. But my mind was twirling. What device had our elderly neighbor used to spy on us? What was it she consistently used to survey the SummerHill area?

Mom's voice disrupted my thoughts. "Isn't it something? In spite of herself, our nosy neighbor had a big part in coming to your aid, Merry." She began to clear the table, carrying teaspoons and Christmasy mugs to the sink.

"Who knows," I said. "Maybe Miss Spindler could help me solve some of the mysteries that keep cropping up around here."

Mom eyed me more seriously. "Better wait till you're back to normal—feeling completely well—before you try cracking another case."

I had to chuckle. "Don't worry, Mom, I'm not physically ready for sleuthing just yet." But in the heart and soul of me, I was.

"Good, because I, for one, have had more than my share of excitement. Enough to last a lifetime."

I agreed and went back to the living room, where Abednego and Lily White—my oldest and youngest cats—joined me a few minutes later. In their own unique way, the felines kept watch over me with an occasional shift of an eyelid at half-mast. It was the cutest thing I'd seen either of them do in a long time.

"Hey, what's with the weepy watch guard?" I teased them, not realizing Mom had followed me into the room.

"There you go again, Merry. You're talking that way again—alliteration style."

I thought back to what I'd just said. "Hey, you're right. I wonder why."

Her eyebrows flew up at the additional *w*'s. This weird way of conversing reminded me of Jon Klein. He'd talked like that in the hospital and on the phone, too. And for some strange reason, he kept trying to get me to speak that way, too. It had something to do with a word game, he'd said. Something from our past maybe?

Although I pondered the situation, it was impossible to come up with a solution. Unless . . .

"Mom, can nearly drowning or a trauma like that alter someone's speech patterns?"

She sat across from me on a chair beside the hearth. Turning to face me, she frowned for a second, then spoke. "Are you worried about it, Merry?"

I shrugged. "It just seems so odd that I would continue to alliterate almost without thinking."

She got up and came over to sit in her prized Boston rocker, handcrafted in the late eighteenth century. "Honey, the human brain is a complex and wondrous creation of God. I honestly don't think you have anything to be worried about. The doctors checked you out thoroughly in the hospital—neurologists, you name it. Your father saw to it that you had the very best doctors in all of Lancaster County."

"So you don't think I'll be alliterating like this the rest of my life?"

She reached for my hand. "We'll pray, if you'd like."

"I've already been talking to the Lord about it," I said. "Told God all about my accident and the awful aimless aggravation—"

"Merry?" Mom had stopped me on purpose. "Take a deep breath and start again."

I groaned. "What'll I do? I mean, what if I keep this up? Alliteration isn't addicting at all, is it?"

The look on my mother's face spelled apprehension.

Sure as anything, she must've thought I'd lost it.

There was only one thing left to do. I must *remember*! I would simply have to make myself remember everything I could about Jonathan Klein and his wacky word game.

FOURTEEN

It was dark by five-fifteen on Christmas Day evening. Mom went around lighting all the candles on the main level of the house. The fireplace mantel was aglow with soft, golden light.

Then after insisting that I bundle up in an afghan and my furriest slippers, Mom was finally satisfied that I was cozy and warm enough to be abandoned briefly while she went to make a light supper.

I thought about Chelsea. Poor girl. Alone this Christmas season without her mom. She'd promised to call and fill me in on the first visit to the rehabilitation center.

But when my friend hadn't called by the time we finished eating the main course, which was mostly leftovers from noon, I began to fret. "It's not like Chelsea," I said as Dad and Skip cleared the table. "She said she'd let me know how things went with her mom last night."

Dad stood behind his chair, pausing to reflect. "Well, I certainly hope there was a counselor on hand when Chelsea and her father visited. The initial face-to-face encounter is often upsetting . . . for all concerned."

I thought for a moment. "Well, I hope everything went okay." Then I remembered the Christmas gift Chelsea had planned to give her mother. "Do you think the pictures I took might've upset Mrs. Davis?"

Dad pulled out his chair and sat down. "You wouldn't think such a thing would be troubling, but in cases like brainwashing—especially those involving a cult—it's often difficult to say what may trigger emotional problems."

Now I was really worried and decided I couldn't wait any longer to talk to Chelsea. As soon as dessert was finished, I'd give her a call.

Mom brought over a tray of coffee for Dad and hot chocolate for Skip and me. She sliced one of the pumpkin pies. "Do you feel up to having sweets?" she asked me, picking up the whipped cream.

Dad grinned and reached across the table, squeezing my elbow. "Bring on the goodies, dear. Our girl is recuperating quickly." He looked at both Skip and me. "We have so much to celebrate this year!"

Skip nodded—one of the first times I'd ever seen him remotely acknowledge that his "little Merry" was worth her salt. My brother's genuine smile warmed me to my croupy soul.

❧   ❧

Once again, I was excused from kitchen cleanup. Hurrying to Dad's study, I closed the door and phoned Chelsea, hoping and praying things were all right with her.

"Hello, Davis residence" came a stiff response.

"Mr. Davis," I said, "this is Merry Hanson calling. May I speak to Chelsea, please?"

"Well, I believe she left to go caroling with some friends. But I'll sure have her return your call."

"Thanks," I said, getting ready to hang up.

"Uh . . . wait just a minute, Merry." He coughed a little. "I heard you took quite a spill on Zooks' pond last weekend. Just wanted to say that I'm mighty glad you're feeling better now."

"Why, thank you, Mr. Davis. That's very kind."

He sighed a bit. "Well, I'll give Chelsea your message when she comes in."

"Okay, and thanks again. Good-bye."

We hung up, and I was surprised at how friendly Mr. Davis had seemed this phone call.

"Everything all right?" Dad asked as I passed him in the hall.

I stopped to tell him what Mr. Davis had said. "But I didn't get any new info on Chelsea's mom. I guess Chelsea's out caroling somewhere."

"Well, don't worry. I'm sure you'll hear something soon." Dad headed for his study, and I went back to enjoy my Christmas gifts in the living room—specifically the new photography books.

While I thumbed through them, I thought about Jon Klein. What was it about him that made me so curious? From what I'd learned of him in the past three days since my accident, he and I shared a whole slew of common interests. But what about *before* my memory lapse? What had gone on between us then?

Speaking in alliterated sentences seemed terribly important to him for some reason—almost a preoccupation. And the more I thought about it, the more baffled I became. But eventually I arrived at a conclusion: I'd interrogate Chelsea, getting her to tell me everything she knew about Jon.

My mind wandered back to the conversation with Chelsea's father. Mr. Davis had said she was out caroling with friends. But my friends were her friends, so why hadn't I heard about this?

The answer came swiftly, almost on wings. The doorbell rang, and when Dad opened it, I heard singing. "Joy to the world, the Lord is come!"

I listened for a moment. The clear sound of Chelsea's soprano voice was evident. So *that's* why I was kept in the dark! Maybe it was intended as a surprise.

Dad called from the foyer. "Merry, some friends of yours are here."

Mom got out of her chair and scurried to the front door to greet them. "Come in, come in," I heard her say. "Merry Christmas to all of you!"

Chelsea and a group of our mutual friends from church came into the living room, greeted me, then went over to stand by the hearth to warm themselves. Soon they were sipping hot chocolate, compliments of Mom, of course.

"We came to cheer you up," Chelsea said, grinning first at me, then at Lissa Vyner, Ashley Horton, Jon Klein, and his sister, Nikki, along with three other teens.

I tossed the afghan aside. Having carolers come indoors on a freezing-cold night, especially when they were dear friends, brightened everything. Especially my outlook. "Happy to have a houseful," I said. "Sing some more songs."

Jon Klein smiled broadly, and I noticed that he turned to Ashley and poked her. "See, that's what I mean. Merry's supreme," he said.

I felt uncomfortable. But Jon's comment didn't seem to bother anyone else. Soon they were singing again— "Angels We Have Heard on High."

Chelsea came over to sit on the throw rug next to the couch. "How are you doing?" she asked as the group continued to sing.

"I'm okay, but what's with Jon?" I whispered.

"Don't freak out," she said, keeping her voice low. "Ashley'll never catch on to his ridiculous game. He thinks you're tops."

I didn't exactly understand what had just happened, but I assumed she'd explain later. What I really wanted to know was how the visit with her mom had been. I was resigned to wait to bring it up, though. Until she and I could talk privately.

The angel song came to a lovely, lilting climax. Dad started the applause. Mom, Skip, and I followed suit.

"What's your favorite carol?" Lissa asked. "Maybe we could sing it for you."

"If all of us know it," Ashley piped up, smiling up at Jon.

"Oh, it's an easy one," I said. "Do you know 'I Heard the Bells on Christmas Day'?"

Jon and two other boys were nodding that they knew it, then tested their baritone and tenor ranges just for fun. Someone said it was getting a bit too toasty by the fire, so they all sat down on the floor while Mom went to find an old hymnal. Ashley and Lissa ended up finding the right pitch for the group, and they began to sing, sharing the hymnal as best they could.

Sonorous but sweet sounds filled the room. They sang mostly in harmony, four part on certain phrases. During the last verse, Mom disappeared from the room again, only to return with two large serving plates of cookies— the snickerdoodles from Miss Spindler and Mom's own specialty, rich chocolate chip.

Chelsea stayed close to me throughout the visit. And in between cookie munching and sips of hot cider, the casual choir of carolers entertained us with a cappella music.

Skip even joined in on several choruses, clowning around with his old girlfriend Nikki Klein, who seemed mighty happy about seeing him again.

All in all, the evening was entirely too short.

"It's getting late," Ashley said, glancing at her watch.

The kids got up and were milling around, some of them going over to ooh and ahh at Mom's splendid angel decorations on the tree.

When Dad offered to drive them back to Chelsea's house, she graciously declined. "Thanks, anyway, but we want to make a quick stop at Miss Spindler's."

"Oh, how thoughtful," Mom said, getting up to collect the empty mugs.

"After Old Hawk Eyes' place, where are you headed?" Skip asked.

Mom looked startled at Miss Spindler's nickname, but Skip wiggled his head comically, grinning back at her. "It's okay, Mom. Really."

Nikki Klein giggled. "You should come along," she invited him.

The twinkle in Skip's eyes gave him away. Going off to college hadn't wiped away his memory of Jon's pixie-faced sister.

"We'll probably end up at the Zooks' house last," Chelsea said. "I want to personally thank Levi Zook for saving Merry's life." She smiled sweetly at me.

When I glanced back at the group, astonishment was written all over Jon Klein's face. He began to rub his chin, looking puzzled. "No one said anything about singing for the Amish," he muttered.

"Oh, you don't have a thing to worry about," my brother said. "The Zooks are some of the nicest people you'll ever meet. Right, Merry?"

Jon glanced at me again at that juncture, as well as Skip. There were big question marks in Jon's eyes, though. Made me nervous.

Ashley—the dear girl—corralled Jon into the hallway just then, where Dad's voice could be heard assisting the carolers with the location of jackets and things.

Chelsea got up and leaned down to speak to me. "Hope you liked the surprise, Mer. Happy Christmas."

"Thanks. It was really great," I said, gazing over my

shoulder. "And especially fun was watching Jon and Ashley together."

"I think he's got an alliteration agenda. Something about that word game of his."

"Really? How do you know?" I said, wondering why I should even care.

She straightened her long sweater. "I overheard Jon saying it was time to teach more of his friends how to speak alliteration-eze."

"Meaning Ashley Horton?" I said. "Think she can do it?"

Chelsea frowned. "Do you remember disliking her . . . from before?"

"I never disliked Ashley. *Never.*" I studied my friend. "Did I?"

Chelsea was nodding her head and making groaning sounds.

"Well, I can't imagine why. I mean, Ashley's got a lot going for her."

Fluffing her auburn locks, Chelsea grabbed my hand. "If you don't get your memory back pretty soon, Mer, she's going to have a lot more going for her!"

I didn't ask her to spell things out. I was sick with a lousy cough and a faulty memory, but I wasn't ignorant.

Evidently, Jon had been someone truly important to me.

In so many words, Chelsea had just said so. And it was high time to find out why!

"Call me the minute you get home," I pleaded. "We have to talk—tonight!"

"I'll call, but don't hold your breath about Ashley. She may not be Jon's intellectual equal, but she likes him. And I mean a lot!"

I almost told her that it didn't matter, that *I* liked Levi Zook . . . a lot. But knowing Chelsea, she'd only remind me that Levi had a call from God to preach. Or something like that.

FIFTEEN

"I really don't know what to tell you about Jon," Chelsea said later when she called. "But I know one thing—before your accident you really liked him. And that's the honest truth."

"What about Levi?" I asked hesitantly.

"I don't think you were all that excited about seeing him this Christmas. I tried my best to read the last part of his last letter, but you snatched it away, like it was private or something."

"There's a letter from Levi? Where?"

"You hid it. Probably with all the others."

I could hardly believe this. "You mean Levi's been writing me? Oh, Chelsea, this is such wonderful news!"

She was groaning now. "Listen, Mer, this entire conversation is really hopeless. I mean, you really can't decide anything about either guy until you get your memory back. Don't you see?"

I didn't want to talk logic. Not now. "So you think I had a crush on Jon, is that it?"

"Think? Girl, I *know* you were nuts about Jon. But

why, I couldn't begin to tell you. Most of the time his head's buried in some book. Grades have always been more important to the guy than girls."

"Hey, have you been practicing Jon's word game?"

She laughed. "Not on your life. That alliteration stuff is for ingenious people."

"Like me?" I laughed. Somehow it relieved the stress.

She didn't answer, though, and I felt very sympathetic toward her when she changed the subject. To her mother and the visit last night. "It was a disaster."

"Oh, Chelsea. I wondered why you didn't call."

"Well, Mom couldn't exactly handle the emotion of seeing either Daddy or me."

"And the pictures? What did she think of them?"

"They made her cry. She could hardly talk to either of us. Like I said, it was awful."

I remembered what my dad had said about a counselor. "Was a professional with you during the visit? Someone to help deal with the transition?"

Chelsea breathed hard into the phone. "There were two advisors present, but none of it seemed to help much. I guess it was just too soon for Mom."

"I'm sorry," I blurted. "We'd all hoped—"

"Please, don't give up, Merry. I'm not."

"That's good, because your mom needs you. I hope you know that."

"It's just so depressing, especially when I had my heart set on something special happening . . . for Christmas."

I could feel her pain, even though I didn't fully understand what she was experiencing. "I'll keep praying, okay?"

"Thanks," she said with tears in her voice.

"I wish you'd told me sooner," I said.

"It wasn't the easiest thing, holding it up inside, but I was worried about *you*, Merry. I nearly lost you. I wouldn't want to say or do anything to make you worse."

"Thanks to Levi, I'm still here."

She laughed a little. "I wish you could've seen him tonight when we caroled over there. Levi kept asking your brother about you after almost every song!"

"You're kidding? In front of everyone?" My neck grew warm envisioning the scene.

"Levi's very unique," she said. "But you have to trust me, Mer, you were far more interested in Jon than Levi."

"Before I fell into the pond?" I moaned. "Oh, what'll I do? My feelings are all so jumbled up."

Chelsea promised to help me regain my memory. "But only when you're ready."

"I'm ready now. Honest!"

She was giggling. "You name the time, and I'll be there."

"We can't do anything about it tomorrow," I said. "My grandparents are coming over from New Jersey. They spent the first part of the holidays with my aunt and uncle."

"I bet they loved seeing your twin baby cousins. How old are they now?"

"Becky and Ben will be seven months old tomorrow. Grandpa and Grandma Landis—my mom's parents—always divide the holidays between Aunt Teri and Uncle Pete, and us."

"Well, I won't push you, Mer, but time's running against us, if you know what I mean."

"We have to keep Jon from linking up with Ashley."

"We have some work to do," she said. "Number one, we've gotta think of something to keep him from giving her alliteration instructions."

"Whatever you say." I smiled into the phone. "And what makes you think you can cure me?"

"For starters, we can always pray about it, right?"

"Always," I said.

"And there's the little matter of your poetry books."

"So?"

"You'll see what I mean." Chelsea seemed so confident. I hoped she was right. Because for once in my life, I realized I was *not* the one being counted on. Miss Fix-It was the one in most need of repair.

❧   ❧

Even though I always thoroughly enjoyed time spent with my grandparents, having them stay with us now was a bit distracting. I needed time to focus on what Chelsea had said—that she wasn't kidding when she declared right down the line that I'd liked Jon. And not so much Levi.

Trust was the key. What else could I do?

I searched high and low for Levi's letters, hoping they might give me some insight into my former feelings.

I started with my desk drawers, searching through

school assignments, old address books, and an occasional note from Jon Klein. Funny, on one of them, I'd penned the nickname "The Alliteration Wizard."

Somehow, though, the title didn't do anything for me—not as far as bringing back the memory I'd lost. And I knew that even if Chelsea had been here, I wouldn't have given the nickname more than a passing glance.

The shelves of my walk-in closet were next on my list. Scouring the colorful shoe boxes and scrapbooks on the first shelf, I found only odds and ends. Nothing pertinent to either Levi or Jonathan.

It was late in the day when I discovered the pinkish box on the middle shelf. I'd come upstairs to get my camera because Mom wanted some close-up shots of Grandpa and Grandma beside the nativity scene in the dining room. That's how I happened onto Levi's letters. Almost half a shoe box full.

Of course, I couldn't just sit there and sift through them with relatives waiting to be photographed. So I set the box on my desk and told my cats to guard it with one of their nine lives.

Grandma was fussing over Grandpa's shirt collar, trying to get it perfectly aligned with his tie, when I arrived. He grumbled about it, glancing over at me every so often until the collar was exactly to Grandma's liking. "Don't you want to look nice for your granddaughter's picture?" she coaxed.

He mumphed and garrumphed, and finally the two of them were posing with broad smiles.

"Don't wear out your smiles just yet." I walked backward around the long table, checking for just the right angle. Leaning on the buffet, I steadied my hand. "Okay, one . . . two . . . three."

Click.

"Now, hold it right there," I said. But I coughed unexpectedly and had to retake.

Mom went to the kitchen to get my evening dose of antibiotics and cough syrup. Then it was time to try for several more shots.

Grandpa was in a bad way by the time I was completely satisfied. In fact, he was pushing his tie loose and unbuttoning the top button on his dress shirt as I put my camera in its case.

Trying not to think about Chelsea, who was probably waiting for a phone call, I joined my family for home videos featuring Ben and Becky. The tiny twins were adorable, and as I watched, I thought back to the day I'd found a baby girl in our backyard—in the gazebo.

"Looks like Becky might be a little bigger than her brother," Mom observed.

"Well, you know how it is with girls," Grandma offered. "They fill out quickly."

Grandpa laughed outright. "They're only babies, for cryin' out loud. Give the little fella some slack."

We chuckled at his comment, and the next time I looked over at Grandpa, he was sound asleep in his chair.

❧   ❧

By the time I dressed for bed, I was too exhausted to bother with all of Levi's letters. My respiratory infection and the worry over my fickle amnesia had worn me out.

But I took time to pray, beginning with Chelsea's mom. "Dear Lord, it would be terribly hard for me to be in my friend's shoes, but you know just what to do to ease her disappointment and pain. And I pray for Mrs. Davis. Please, will you help her adjust to the idea of coming home . . . and soon? Chelsea and her father really need her. They want her with them."

I continued on, praying that in God's perfect time and way I would remember the things I needed to know about my life. "Not just because there might be some cute boy involved, Lord. But I ask this because I'm your child and I know you love me. Amen."

Maybe tomorrow things would clear up for me. If not, I'd keep trusting. It was the only way.

SIXTEEN

First thing, even before I showered, I read Levi's letters. Every last one of them. Wow, what an expressive guy! And from reading them, I could tell that he was determined and directed. Knew what he wanted. Maybe *that's* what I liked so much about him.

Chelsea had been absolutely right—Levi had his sights set on me. Oh, glory! But if what she'd said about my former feelings—if all that was accurate—I wasn't supposed to be overjoyed about it. I had to keep telling myself that Jon was the boy the pre-accident Merry had liked. *He* was the boy of my dreams.

Such a mix-up, not to understand your own feelings.

I got out of bed, sweet-talking my cats into coming downstairs with me for their breakfast. Mom and Grandma were already up scrambling eggs and making Belgian waffles—on the new waffle iron Mom had received for Christmas.

"Hope you're hungry," she said, coming over to see for herself how I was doing today.

"I hardly coughed all night," I told her. "The medicine must be working."

I caught her studying me. "Something else is working, too." Mom smirked a bit. "You're not alliterating."

"I'm not?"

She nodded. "I think it may be a good sign."

"Maybe my memory's mending."

She grinned. "Meaning?"

I laughed. "Mom, you're amazing. Wait'll I tell Jon Klein about you."

She waved her hand with a smile and went to help Grandma with breakfast.

❧   ❧

Chelsea and I had the most remarkable fun together that afternoon. Actually, what she had in mind was quite revealing.

She stood comically in the center of my large bedroom, just the way I had last week when I'd read out of my poetry book. "Okay, here's what we're going to do," she said, sitting me down on my desk chair, facing her. "Don't say anything, Mer, just listen." She pulled out a piece of paper, turning it so that I could see the long list of things she'd written.

"I'm listening." I snuggled with Lily White.

"This is a list of memory starters," Chelsea began.

Squelching a snicker, I pretended to be impressed. "Go ahead—trigger my brain."

"C'mon, this is serious stuff." She put one hand on her hip and began. "Last week, when you and I visited

Rachel Zook—that's Levi's sister, in case you forgot—she invited you to her surprise skating party when we were upstairs in her bedroom. She wanted you to come and be Levi's partner, and you said, 'Maybe he should have a say about it,' or some such thing. Anyway, for a little while, I thought you were going to say no, but then Rachel spoke up. 'Do it for Levi,' she said."

"*You* must have a good memory," I said. "Thanks for doing this, Chelsea. I'm enjoying myself."

She shrugged, apparently not too pleased that the first thing on her list hadn't worked an immediate miracle. "Okay, moving on. How about this? Way back as long as I can remember, you've watched out the school bus window, probably watching for Levi when we rode past the Zooks' cornfield. And most every time I'd tease you with something like, 'You must want to hand sew all your clothes or go without electricity all your life.' " She paused a bit, waiting for a reaction from me. "Does that do anything for you, Mer?"

"Nope." I sat very still, trying not to giggle.

She surveyed her long list. "Here's one that just might stir up something: number three. This one's about Jon Klein. And once again, last week you and I were discussing him right here in this very room. Anyway, I told you that it looked like you were soaking up whatever he was saying each day at your locker. And you said—and I quote—'Aren't friends supposed to pay attention to each other?' End of quote."

I couldn't help it; I let out a giggle. "This is so weird listening to you document my every movement—everything I say. It's like you're a walking diary—of *my* life!"

Chelsea flopped down on my bed, obviously not because things were funny. Clearly, she was discouraged. "What are we gonna do, Mer? Don't you see—I'm doing all this for you? So you won't freak out when you regain your faculties but have lost your . . . your . . ."

"My boyfriend?" I asked.

She sat up abruptly. "Oh, I don't know, maybe we're not supposed to force things like this."

"No, wait a minute." I thought of something I'd written about Jon Klein. "Here, let me show you this." Pulling out my desk drawer, I found the note from Jon, where I'd written the nickname for him on the back.

Peering over my shoulder, she read *The Alliteration Wizard*. "Hey, we might be on to something. I mean, if you thought enough of his . . . uh, abilities to alliterate or whatever, and—well, you know—had him on some kind of pedestal about it . . . maybe, just maybe, the crush you had on him has something to do with the word game." She eyed me ruthlessly. "Maybe *that's* what you two were always doing at your locker—talking in your bizarre language."

Then, before I could reply, she started getting all hyped up about it. "Yes! I think we're getting closer to the truth, Mer." She snatched up her list from the bed and scanned it. "Here we go. This is another item about Jon Klein. Now, listen carefully."

"What else can I do?" I teased. "I'm stuck in my own house. I can't go anywhere, right?"

She started reading off something about Jon's sudden

interest in photography. "If it's any consolation to you, you'd be flying high if you were in your . . . uh, right mind, I guess you could say. Don't you see? This must be a major breakthrough—Jon wanting a camera like yours."

We threw the idea around a bit more. And I let Chelsea go on and on about how she really thought that when my memory finally returned I should probably forget about Jon. "Remember I told you once—on the bus, I think—why bother with someone who scarcely knows you exist?"

"But if he wanted a camera like mine . . . what about that?" I asked.

Chelsea got up and went to the window. "Maybe you're right. Maybe things are changing with Jon, who knows?" She stood there, staring out at the snow and ice. "You know, I haven't forgotten that verse by Longfellow—the one you read to me last week."

I got up and went to the corner bookcase and started pulling classic poetry books out. Piling them up, I set them down in front of Chelsea on my bed. "Here you go. Which one?"

"So you don't remember reading about the echoes?"

"Oh, *that* one," I said. "I almost know it by heart." Quickly, I found the page. "Want me to read it to you?"

"Sure, go ahead."

" 'And, when the echoes had ceased, like a sense of pain was the silence.' " I handed her the open book.

A car horn sounded out front. Chelsea got a queer look on her face, and she ran to the window. "It's Daddy," she said. "What's he doing here so soon?"

"Better go see," I said, joining her at the window. "It might be about your mother."

She turned to me. "You might be right. Oh . . . I hope it's not more bad news." And with that, she scurried out of the room and down the steps.

I lingered at the window, watching as Chelsea ran to her father's waiting car. She stopped momentarily to look up and wave, and I waved back.

Curious about my friend's situation, yet feeling quite tired and a bit overwhelmed, I pulled my blue-striped comforter back and crawled into bed for a nap.

In the distance, I heard a midday train whistle twice, echoing across hundreds of acres of slumbering farmland. Straining, I listened as its mournful wail died away.

He will call upon me, and I will answer him. . . .

I imagined the train, going who knows where, rumbling over hills and through valleys. Speeding toward the horizon and beyond. Who was riding today? Where were the people going? Where had they been?

I will be with him in trouble. . . .

I felt as if I would fall asleep any minute. Maybe I already was.

I will deliver him and honor him. . . .

In the heaviness before sleep actually takes place, I thought I heard the creaking sound of the windmill behind Zooks' barn—and saw the outline of bare trees toward the east. Far, far across the frozen pond, where "cellar" holes gobble up lost girls.

And for the first time since my fall through the ice, my past blended with the present.

I remembered.

Seventeen

When I awoke, I pulled the comforter off my bed and wrapped it around me. I sat quietly near the window, letting two of my cats rub against my ankles.

"Jon Klein's hung up on having an alliteration partner, whether it's me or someone else," I said to the cats. I felt a little sad realizing the truth.

But there was hope, I decided. After all, Jon probably hadn't wanted the same kind of camera equipment as mine for nothing. Time would tell about that.

Meanwhile, I'd just have to let him know next time he called—alliteration-eze didn't have to be an exclusive thing between us. That way I'd let him off the hook. In fact, if I were to admit it, it would be kind of fun to get all the kids in our youth group talking that way.

Even Ashley Horton, bless her heart. Given the opportunity and training, of course, she might become very adept at the word game. Depending on her teacher.

I went down the hall to Skip's room, my comforter dragging like a royal train behind me. He was out, probably with Nikki Klein again, but that was all right. Life was too short not to be with your friends whenever possible.

I reached for the phone on my brother's desk.

When Ashley answered the phone, she seemed quite surprised to hear from me. "Hi, Merry. It seems like forever since we really talked."

"Since the photography contest at school," I volunteered.

"So how're you doing?"

"Well, I wish I could tell you just how truly terrific I'm feeling, especially now."

"Oh? Something happen?" She sounded excited and eager.

"You're the very first person to hear about this. I've regained my memory."

"That's great, Merry. Did it happen today?"

"Just a little while ago. I was resting, and the Lord brought everything back to me. Clear as . . . as ice."

She laughed. "I'm sure Jon and the others will be thrilled. I know I am."

I inhaled quickly. "Would you mind letting Jon know about it—that is, if you happen to talk to him before I do?"

"I'd be happy to tell him. In fact, I'll probably see him on New Year's Eve at the church. I hope you'll feel up to coming."

I knew what she was talking about. Every year the youth pastor put together a special "Farewell Service," which included a Bible study, prayer time, and lots of special music. We usually finished up the old year on our knees in prayer.

"Well, I'll have to see what my parents think, but maybe it'll work out for me to come."

"Great," she said, then paused before going on. "Uh . . . Merry, could I ask you a question? It's about Jon's word game—alliteration-eze, I believe he calls it."

"Sure. What do you want to know?" I said, not feeling the least bit intimidated now.

"How hard is it to talk that way?"

"To be honest, Ashley, if you practice, you should be able to catch on pretty fast."

"Really?"

"Sounds like it's important to you." *Like it is to Jon*, I thought.

She laughed softly. "It's a challenge—that's all, really. Most people think I'm a little dense. Maybe if I can do this, like Jon and you do, maybe it'll stretch my mind. You know what I mean?"

Now I was the one chuckling. "Sure, Ashley, I know exactly what you mean. And I know just the person to help you get the hang of it."

"Really? Are you saying *you'll* help me?"

I reached down to stroke Lily White. "Won't Jon be surprised?"

"Maybe we can outdo him someday," Ashley said.

I switched the phone to my left ear. "That's exactly what I had in mind."

She laughed, and I knew this was a genius idea!

Chelsea called right after supper. "You'll never guess what," she said the minute I answered the phone.

"I hope this has something to do with your mom."

"She's home, Merry! My mom's sitting right here in our living room."

"You're kidding! This is fantastic. What happened to make her change her mind?"

Chelsea was chuckling like a little child. "Your pictures, Mer. She kept looking at them after we left on Christmas Eve. And something started working on her heart, and after a few days, she really began to miss Daddy and me. She missed us so much that she convinced her therapist and doctors to allow us to come for another visit."

"And that's where you were going when your dad stopped by this afternoon?"

"Oh, I can't believe this is happening," she said. "It's absolutely the best possible New Year's gift."

"I'm truly happy for you, Chelsea." Then after we discussed all the details of her mother's return, I told her *my* news.

"I remember everything!" I announced.

She couldn't stop talking about it. "Do you think maybe all that reminiscing we did together—you know, my list and everything—do you think it might've helped?"

"Oh, I'm sure it did. So did your prayers."

"It's really special when friends can do something like this for each other," she said. "Your idea about taking pictures of me for my mom sparked something deep in her and . . . well, you know what I'm trying to say, don't you?"

I knew. We'd touched each other's lives in a powerful, meaningful way. Our fondness for each other had literally crisscrossed.

⚜   ⚜

As it turned out, I did get to go for a short time to the New Year's Eve service at church. Mom made sure I was bundled up, and Dad drove me into town with the car heater going full blast.

Jon, Lissa, Ashley, and all the others congratulated me on being well enough to show up.

"Lookin' like lots of lively links to our language." Jon glanced around at the group. "Everyone's eager to exercise energy and—"

"You just wait," I interrupted, referring to Ashley's and my secret plan to outwit him. Boy, was the Alliteration Wizard in for it!

"Aha, do I detect a duel, dear Merry?"

My heart didn't do a single somersault. I stood tall and said, friend to friend, "We'll have a contest very soon."

And grinning with delight, Jon motioned for me to sit with him for the devotional, which I did.

⚜   ⚜

The next day, the first of the New Year, I spent part of the afternoon with Rachel Zook and her younger brother and sisters; Levi too. He took me for a short ride in his car, and while we rode we communicated.

It wasn't akin to alliteration-eze, but a language that has been universal since the beginning of time. We sang—in two-part harmony—mostly Christmas carols. It seemed like a fun thing to do, especially since I'd missed out on the caroling around SummerHill. And Levi had missed out on singing in harmony most of his life because of his Amish upbringing.

"It's wonderful-gut seein' ya all smiles again, Merry," he said, turning into their long lane.

"And I'm very glad you came home for Christmas, Levi," I said, returning his smile.

There was no reaching for my hand or anything else romantic. Levi stopped the car and turned to look at me. "You and I must go ice skating before I go back to Virginia to school. Jah?"

I gasped. "Oh, I don't think so."

He nodded thoughtfully. "That's what people often say after a car wreck, too. But ya can't be waitin' much longer, Merry. You need to get back on your skates."

I had all sorts of excuses, though. "My skates are completely ruined."

"Aw, such a shame," he joked. "We'll just hafta see 'bout that."

Like I always said, Levi was persistent. Never gave up. And because he was stubborn this time, I got my courage back. And much more.

The winter sun was high a week later when Levi knelt to lace up my brand-new skates. "Let's just say they're a gift from an old friend." He grinned up at me.

The first few steps on the ice frightened me nearly to death, but Levi reached for my hand. Then supporting my back, he pushed forward, sending the two of us gliding across the pond. Together.

The wind was gentle and kind on my face this day. And far away were the echoes of fear, growing more distant with each stroke of our skates.

❧　❧

When Levi left for his Mennonite college, I said goodbye with only a touch of sadness. It won't be long—he'll be back for spring break. And there'll be letters . . . plenty of them from both of us.

Chelsea remembered to take her puppy, Secrets, for a visit to his cocker spaniel mama. Little Susie Zook was tickled to see the beautiful gold-haired pup again.

Mrs. Davis is acclimating to her own home and surroundings surprisingly well, and according to Chelsea, she hopes to plant an extra-large flower garden come spring.

As for Jon, the way I view him has begun to change. A brush with death often alters things between friends. For the better, I believe. He's asked me to show him some of the features on my camera—same as his. He could probably figure it out if he read the instruction booklet, but maybe this is the start of a new kind of bond between us.

And Ashley Horton? She and I are planning a big sleepover on Valentine's Day with Chelsea and Lissa—complete with a lesson in alliteration-eze. It's about time the women of SummerHill unite.

Speaking of the neighborhood, Miss Spindler just might be pleased to know that I'm offering my services to house-sit the next time she leaves town. The way I see it, someone's got to get to the bottom of things over there. I mean, how *does* she do it—keeping track of everything and everyone?

Chelsea's offered to help me snoop around—that is, if I ever get inside Old Hawk Eyes' house. Meanwhile, I may have to be content with my imagination. Not an easy task. Especially for a girl who hears echoes in the wind.

From Beverly ... To You

❧   ❧

I'm delighted that you're reading SUMMERHILL SECRETS. Merry Hanson is such a fascinating character—I can't begin to count the times I laughed while writing her humorous scenes. And I must admit, I always cry with her.

Not so long ago, I was Merry's age, growing up in Lancaster County, the home of the Pennsylvania Dutch—my birthplace. My grandma Buchwalter was Mennonite, as were many of my mother's aunts, uncles, and cousins. Some of my school friends were also Mennonite, so my interest and appreciation for the "plain" folk began early.

It is they, the Mennonite and Amish people—farmers, carpenters, blacksmiths, shopkeepers, quiltmakers, teachers, schoolchildren, and bed and breakfast owners—who best assisted me with the research for this series. Even though I have kept their identity private, I am thankful for these wonderfully honest and helpful friends.

If you want to learn more about Rachel Zook and her people, ask for my Amish bibliography when you write. I'll send you the book list along with my latest newsletter. Please include a *self-addressed, stamped envelope* for all correspondence. Thanks!

Beverly Lewis
%Bethany House Publishers
11300 Hampshire Ave. S.
Minneapolis, MN 55438

Teen Series From
Bethany House Publishers

❊❊❊

Early Teen Fiction (11–14)

HIGH HURDLES by Lauraine Snelling
Show jumper DJ Randall strives to defy the odds and achieve her dream of winning Olympic Gold.

SUMMERHILL SECRETS by Beverly Lewis
Fun-loving Merry Hanson encounters mystery and excitement in Pennsylvania's Amish country.

THE TIME NAVIGATORS by Gilbert Morris
Travel back in time with Danny and Dixie as they explore unforgettable moments in history.

Young Adult Fiction (12 and up)

CEDAR RIVER DAYDREAMS by Judy Baer
Experience the challenges and excitement of high school life with Lexi Leighton and her friends—over one million books sold!

GOLDEN FILLY SERIES by Lauraine Snelling
Readers are in for an exhilarating ride as Tricia Evanston races to become the first female jockey to win the sought-after Triple Crown.

JENNIE MCGRADY MYSTERIES by Patricia Rushford
A contemporary Nancy Drew, Jennie McGrady's sleuthing talents promise to keep readers on the edge of their seats.

LIVE! FROM BRENTWOOD HIGH by Judy Baer
When eight teenagers invade the newsroom, the result is an action-packed teen-run news show exploring the love, laughter, and tears of high school life.

THE SPECTRUM CHRONICLES by Thomas Locke
Adventure and romance await readers in this fantasy series set in another place and time.

SPRINGSONG BOOKS by various authors
Compelling love stories and contemporary themes promise to capture the hearts of readers.

WHITE DOVE ROMANCES by Yvonne Lehman
Romance, suspense, and fast-paced action for teens committed to finding pure love.

9608